Praise for Lee Murray

"*Despatches* is all at once heart-breaking and mythic, highlighting one of the darkest chapters in human history. Murray presents truth and fiction simultaneously, putting the reader amongst the horrors, both real and imagined."

— Greg Chapman, Bram Stoker Award® and Australian Shadows Award-nominated author

"Multi-award-winning author Lee Murray skilfully combines history, horror, and Māori mythology to create a gripping tale that will slither its way into your imagination, there to make its dark, abiding lair."

— Anna Taborska, author of *Bloody Britain* and *For Those Who Dream Monsters*

"Lee Murray's *Despatches* innovates the Lovecraftian with her signature chills in an enthralling epistolary tale of compassion and eldritch horrors set during one of the bloodiest campaigns of World War One."

— CRAIG DILOUIE, AUTHOR OF *EPISODE THIRTEEN*

"What imagined terrors can rival the all-too-human horror of war? In the powerfully melancholy *Despatches*, Lee Murray offers both, pitching the distressingly real theatre of blood and carnage as a cosmic board for a mythic game between gods beyond our comprehension, playing with people like pawns. And one truth pervades it all – no one wins here. This is historical horror fiction at its most beguiling."

— ALAN BAXTER, AWARD-WINNING AUTHOR OF *THE GULP* AND *SALLOW BEND*

"Death, disfigurement, and disease prowl the battlelines at Gallipoli, slaughtering men in their thousands. But soon there will be more to fear than the enemy. Within the fetid trenches and freezing coastal waters, an ancient evil will be drawn to the chaos. Blending fact and fiction, *Despatches* leaves the reader with a distinct feeling of unease and sorrow. Another masterful tale from Lee Murray."

— ALISTER HODGE, INTERNATIONAL BESTSELLING AUTHOR, AUREALIS AND AUSTRALASIAN SHADOWS AWARD FINALIST

"A masterclass in weaving myth into the darkest gaps in history, Lee Murray's latest novella is at once moving and disturbing. Murray's writing breathes life to the very human face of the Allied Campaign and conjures terrifying cosmic forces that lie behind the madness of war. Among the mud, despair, and death, there are aching moments of connection and ordinary beauty, which hold a bittersweet light against the realisation we are ultimately small and alone against the pitiless dark. Meticulously researched and vividly written, *Despatches* is outstanding historical horror."

— GENEVE FLYNN, DOUBLE BRAM
STOKER AWARD-WINNER, AND EDITOR
OF *BLACK CRANES*

"Horror is a good match for war: wouldn't we rather believe in the fantastical than the brutal insanity of combat? Lee Murray's *Despatches* wraps the all-too-real horror of the Dardanelles campaign in a gossamer of eldritch fancies, creating a story that is not only a superb piece of historical fiction but a damned good horror story, too."

— ALMA KATSU, AUTHOR OF *THE
FERVOR*

"Murray's *Despatches* has all the hallmarks of a classic; capturing not only the imagination, but the strengths and failings of what it is to be human."

— DAVE JEFFERY, AWARD-WINNING AUTHOR OF THE *A QUIET APOCALYPSE* SERIES

DESPATCHES

LEE MURRAY

ISBNs:
978-1-0670158-0-0 (print)
978-1-0670158-1-7 (ebook)

Despatches was first published by PS Publishing, UK, September 2023

"Edward's Journal" was first published in *Cthuhlu Land of the Long White Cloud*, Steve Proposch, Christopher Sequiera, and Bryce Stevens (eds.), IFWG, Australia, 2018

Squabbling Sparrows Press

For Len Nicklin

ACKNOWLEDGMENTS

I've always imagined the acknowledgments section of a book as a kind of private awards show—*sans* golden trophies and sequinned gowns—where the author pulls back the velvet curtain to celebrate all the people who have helped behind the scenes, people who have inspired them or enriched the work in some way. So I would like to raise my glass to writers Angela Yuriko Smith, Maxwell Ian Gold, and Linda Dawley, who commented on early drafts of *Despatches*, and blow kisses to Robbie Murray for his infectious passion for history and his willingness to chat at length with his mum about the Allied campaign of 1915—or any odd historical fact. I'm grateful to my talented editor and friend, Marie O'Regan, for her help in polishing the story, and to my colleagues at Squabbling Sparrows Press for giving this edition a home. Special thanks to artist Greg Chapman for the cover, and to the kind colleagues who offered their endorsements. I thank you all for your support. Imaginary bouquets are on their way.

Despatches

Cassius Smythe, telegram to John Edward Ritter, 7th Division, British Expeditionary Forces, 2 April 1915

John.
> Gone to the Dardanelles with sturdy pair boots.
> Your very good friend, Cassius.

Cassius Smythe, journal entry, April 1915

John, I am aboard a transport ship, entering Homer's Aegean Sea in early spring. I wish dearly that you could see it. Perhaps one day, when this Great War is over, we might journey here together. I shall hope for that. For now, let me tell you that the sky is vast, and the sea is an uncanny blue. Although I do not care for the rocking of the craft, which pained me greatly on the voyage, the sight of the bay is worth a little nausea as it is as beautiful and idyllic as our history books implied. Truly a crucible for the gods.

The reason for our presence, however, is far from serene. The failure of the Empire's naval forces to reach the Ottoman stronghold of Constantinople has prompted Asquith and his government—influenced by the opinion of Admiral Churchill—to launch a land offensive on the Dardanelle Peninsula. You may have already heard of the campaign as the Dominion has made no secret of its plans. I fear the Turks have heard it too and are even now rallying their army to reinforce the border. After all, they have an entire country at their back and every incentive to keep us, the invaders, out. As I gaze out over this beguiling sea, I am reminded that despite the current calm, these waters have already claimed the *Bouvet* and the *Irresistible*, the destroyers sunk just weeks ago by Ottoman mines. I shudder to think that those horrors might drift beneath me even now.

Little surprise then that I am full of a mix of the excitement and disquiet you described to me before your departure when we were last together. All about me the mood of the men, many of whom are barely out of short trousers, is tense. The air is fair humming with it. Perhaps it is always this way on the eve of battle.

I wonder where you are and how you are faring, my dearest friend. The news reports from the Western Front and England's conquests there are heartening, so I shall hope for the best.

Cassius Smythe, letter to Emma Violet Smythe of Bexley Heath, Kent, April 1915

Dear Mother,

Rest assured, I am *sain et sauf,* despite my dire lack of correspondence. I am joined with the Mediterranean Expeditionary Forces, stationed with my journalist colleagues on the island of [redacted] in the Aegean, the staging post for the battle between the Ottoman and British empires. Can you believe it? Your son, tasked with reporting on the glorious events leading to the Dominion's inevitable control of the Dardanelle Peninsula. At least, I cannot complain at the lack of adventure!

I am sorry, however, not to have been able to write you sooner; indeed, I scarce had time to pack my typewriter before I embarked from London, although the apparatus has suffered greatly in the voyage. The leather case, already scratched and battered, is now so much the worse for wear, and for the most part I am resigned to pencil and paper. The isle itself is picturesque, the craggy hills at our back, painted in hues of gold and lilac, breathtaking in spite of the circumstances of our location. The inhabitants, simple fishermen and goat farmers most, are vastly outnumbered by our expeditionary forces, some [redacted] [redacted] of them, soldiers from all over the world, including Australians and Māorilanders, known to all as Anzacs, who are arrived fresh from training in the deserts of [redacted].

The campaign, though, looks set to be a short one. The seas are simply churning with our ships. From their positions on the clifftops, the Turks must tremble at the sight of them. Certainly, the officers of the *Entente* are optimistic, convinced we will capture the Peninsula with ease, and from there push on to take [redacted] by Christmas. All at once I am thinking of the Christmas pudding you served when I last saw you. Please kiss Harriet for me. I expect she is a young lady now and far too grown up to spare a kiss for her brother. If you are able, please extend my regards to Father, too. Tell him that I carry no ill will, never mind the violent discourse of our last meeting.

I will write again as soon as I can. Perhaps, before you receive my next missive, you will read of my adventures in my reports for the London *Daily Star*.

Your son, Cassius.

Cassius Smythe, journal entry, 25 April 1915

John, I can barely write for the quake of my hands and the blurring of my eyes, yet out of honour and respect for the brave men who fell in the first hours of this campaign and for those still forging their way up treacherous precipices under enemy fire, I am determined to record the events of the past two days while they remain fresh in my mind. First, I must tell you that I was, and am still, at a safe distance from the fray, beyond the reach of the Ottoman guns aboard a hospital ship, just one of a flotilla of Allied craft on this sea of legend. Most of my account has been gleaned from those men carrying the casualties, since the troops themselves were, for the most part, mutilated beyond words. For the rest, these were observations made from the deck, either with my naked eye or with the aid of a telescope, and padded with intelligence widely known to those associated with the campaign.

The land attack on the Turkish peninsula was made in three separate landings, with the British and French leading the main assault at Cape Helles, and the less experienced Australian and New Zealand forces landing further north at Gaba Tepe. I was with the Anzacs, although, as I said, only at a distance.

It was scarcely four a.m. when the first troop boats set out, and in those early moments, the air hung with anticipation, salt, and the soft whisper of thyme. The landing was slow: while the Australian divisions snaked away in the grey light of dawn, night had long fallen by the time the last of the New Zealanders set foot on the peninsula. The time that passed in between the first and last man can only be described as chaotic and deadly. No sooner had the diggers swung their legs over the side of the boats than they were mowed down by Turkish troops who held the higher ground and who riddled the water, the beach, and the hillside with a hail of gunfire. Nor was there any cover for our men on the steep precipices and ravines that towered over a stretch of beach barely twenty-five yards wide. By all accounts, it was a riot. The noise was deafening, with our own HMS *Queen Elizabeth* and the HMS *Majestic* firing on the hills with their impressive batteries. On the ground, divisions were mixed and men misplaced in the confusion; the route was narrow, under fire, and mined in places; and vital equipment was late arriving (from picks and shovels to artillery and guns). And while each man carried ninety pounds of equipment on his person, many abandoned their packs and necessary equipment on the slopes in favour of speed.

Apparently, the Anzacs had been ordered to take the strategic hill of Mal Tepe a mile inland, yet none of the officers, nor anyone else for that matter, appeared to have been told exactly how they might achieve that. Names like Shrapnel Hill and Death Valley and the like were bandied about. I have yet to locate a map to determine where these might be, but wherever they are, it is clear from the reports, and the ragged remains of the men who have returned, that we have sent our boys into hell itself.

Cassius Smythe, journal entry, April 1915

I submitted my report of the landing. The Navy censors refuse to send it on to the offices of the *Daily Star*, reminding me that the press corps are here at Gallipoli and its environs on the sufferance of the War Office. My article, it seems, would not be good for morale. Indeed. I do not imagine many young men would rush to the arena if they knew they would likely have their heads blown off mere hours, or worse, minutes, after disembarking. Since I am a civilian, I am *requested* rather than ordered to please rewrite my article, this time representing the Empire in more gracious terms.

The Times, *London, Greater London, England, Tuesday 27 April 1915*

COAST BATTLE IN THE BALANCE
[267th day of war]

The army of the Allies landed at various points on the Gallipoli Peninsula on Sunday, and the general attack on the Dardanelles by the fleet and army has been resumed. The Admiralty and War Office issued a joint statement last night announcing this. The landing of the army began before sunrise on Sunday. It met with serious opposition. The enemy was posted in strong entrenchments protected by barbed wire. Nevertheless, the landing was completely successful. Before nightfall, large forces were established on shore.[1*]

---

* 1. "Coast Battle in the Balance", *The Times*, London, Greater London, England, Tuesday 27 April 1915. https://www.newspapers.com/topics/world-war1/gallipoli-campaign/

Cassius Smythe, journal entry, May 1915

John, I have been privy to Ellis Ashmead-Bartlett's letter on the "Expedition to the Dardanelles" which he intends for Asquith himself. Ashmead-Bartlett, a veteran war correspondent and a darling of Fleet Street, is one of the boldest fellows I have ever had the occasion to meet. Can you believe he went to Anzac Cove himself on landing day, disembarking with the New Zealanders, and was arrested on suspicion of being a spy! If it were not for the testimony of a seaman who had seen him arrive, he might have been shot.

For all his extravagance, the man has a way with words. He has enlisted the help of Australian newsman Murdoch, newly arrived, to help him smuggle his writings to London by way of Egypt. Ellis has a politician's guile, rubbed off from his pater no doubt, and he is just arrogant enough to get away with it. He has no choice, of course, as it is certain the Official Press Bureau (indulge me if I join my colleagues in calling it the *Suppress Bureau*) will not allow anything he has written to reach the esteemed offices of the *Telegraph*. Probably a good thing as it could earn him life imprisonment, or at the very least a hefty fine, and all the world knows the man is already a bankrupt.

While A-B is far too much of a dandy for my liking, dear John, I admire his gall, and despite the flamboyance of his prose and his person, his account of the campaign is the closest to the truth that I have read, although it does not tell the whole of it.

Cassius Smythe, journal entry, May 1915

Since there is no point in attempting to get my accounts of the skirmishes and *enfilades*, the terrifying back and forth of gunfire, passed through the censors—they would not succeed without a spiderweb of black markings that would render them senseless—I have turned my attention instead to recording the personal testimonies of the men of the campaign: soldiers, chaplains, snipers, stretcher bearers, all in the hope of providing as true an account as possible of life here in the midst of war. By rights, we of the press are restricted in our access to the troops or the front line by courtesy of the Military, but Ellis Ashmead-Bartlett is of the opinion we should go where we please and ask forgiveness later. I will follow this advice rather than remain ensconced at Imbros (where some of the press have settled in for the duration, planning to spend the rest of the campaign drinking wine and partaking of the food prepared by A-B's personal chef). To that end, I will concentrate my investigations at Anzac Cove, and, on occasion elsewhere, making necessary use of the Allies' trawlers, hospital ships, mules, and other transportation to travel to those destinations of interest.

Cassius Smythe, journal entry, late May 1915

I was fortunate to secure an interview with a seaman, a Jack Tar as they are called here, and not just any seaman: Thomas Harding is a surviving crew member of the HMS *Triumph*, which was sunk by a German U-21 submarine torpedo off the coast of Saffros Bay (Gaba Tepe) on the 25th of May.

I'd seen the battleship go down myself from my dugout near the beach at Anzac Cove, and it was a sorry sight indeed. While providing bombardment support to troops on the ridge, the *Triumph* was hit on the starboard side by a torpedo. The explosion caused her to list to the portside, the list becoming more dramatic over several agonising minutes, until eventually, she flipped over like a teacup put to drain on the rack. Less than a half-hour after being hit she was gone to the bottom of the sea, taking seventy-five poor souls with her. The survivors, plucked from the boats, and some from the water, were rescued by the HMS *Nelson*. Here, below, is a *précis* of my interview with Harding and his crewman, a man named Johnson:

"There was a to-do on board after the torpedo hit.

Men were running every which way. Getting to the boats. We knew the drill, but this was the real thing, so it was quite thrilling. The boat was listing considerably by the time I got to the deck. We lowered as many boats as we could before she got too far, but some of the crew didn't make it. It hurt my heart to see the *Triumph* go down all guns blazing.

"Since the German submarine that hit us was still in the vicinity, Allied ships didn't dare approach us to pick us up, so we had to wait a while to be rescued, which gave us some tense moments, I can tell you. Then, finally, the HMS *Nelson* retrieved us, and we were on board there for a while. They warmed us up and looked after us. It was a sad thing to lose the *Triumph*. I'm told the morale of the whole Peninsula went down with her, and the HMS *Majestic* soon after, so it was a bad few days for the Empire. Jacko might have taken the chance to push his advantage, but it seemed even the Turks lowered their guns when the old girl went under. Out of respect, I guess."

I read aloud from my notebook, reciting Harding's words back at him. "She went down all guns blazing, even overturned as she was . . . What would have caused those still on board to do that?"

Harding paused as if reflecting on something, then said, "I wasn't on board, Mr Smythe, so I couldn't rightly tell you what was in their minds, but some of those on the lifeboats say it was because the U-21 was hiding under the *Triumph* to escape notice of the nearby warships."

I sensed the man was holding something back. "The submarine was hovering under the sinking ship, you say? That's a bold move, isn't it? One that would take some skill."

Hunkered alongside me, Harding gazed out of the dugout and over the bay. "Those men were our friends. Heroes, every one. Even with their lives forfeit, they would not have given up on those of us in the water. They would have attacked the submarine to their very last breath."

The other man, Johnson, had been hovering at the entrance to the dugout listening to our conversation. Shouldering Harding aside, he crouched and said, "It's true they were heroes, but they weren't firing on the submarine."

"Johnson," Harding started, as he recovered his crouched position, but the seaman stilled him with a look.

"It isn't honest, Tom, and you know it." Johnson turned to me. "The *Triumph* went down all guns blazing because there was something under her, that's true. But it wasn't the sub. From the lifeboats, we all saw the U-boat dive, watched her speed away. The *Triumph* was done for, and the sub was getting out of there as fast as she could. Instead, it was a colossal sea creature that passed under the ship and circled around us. We all saw it. Tom included."

"We saw a *shadow*," Harding insisted, "and a long way below us. It was a grey day. It might have been a cloud. Or a whale."

"I've seen plenty of whales," Johnson said. "It wasn't a whale."

Seated on a crate, I leaned forward, my journal on my knees, and did my best to keep my voice even. "Could you describe this sea creature for me, Mr Johnson?"

"It was like a serpent, only it was so big it could have swallowed a lifeboat and everyone in it."

I hadn't meant to shake my head, but it was quite the story.

"He doesn't believe you, Glen. Come away." Pulling on his friend's arm, Harding got to his feet. Johnson shrugged him off.

"I'm sorry," I said. "It's just . . . And you say everyone in the boats saw it?"

Harding's nod acknowledged Johnson's version of events. "All of us who were not injured saw it, although few will swear to it. I reckon those left on board the *Triumph*, the ones who couldn't get off the vessel, saw that monster circling us and they fired off the guns to save us," he said. "I think they got it, too, took it to the bottom of the sea with them, because after the *Triumph* disappeared, we didn't see it again."

"Do you know how many ships we've lost to this sea?" Johnson said.

"I don't—"

Harding said, "Too many, Mr Smythe. It's not just

the war; there's something else out there." He exhaled deeply, as if relieved to have the burden lifted from his shoulders.

"We thought maybe you could write it in the papers," Johnson said hopefully.

John, I didn't know what to tell them. Mr Gardiner at the *Daily Star* would not be happy to read of it. Easier to say the ship went down to enemy fire and leave it at that.

I told them I would see what I could do.

***

Cassius Smythe, excerpt of an article in the Daily Star *characters of the campaign series, May 1915*

THE HARDY SAPPER

The sapper is an engineer who provides vital support for our brave men fighting the Turk on the Dardanelle coast. From the French "sappe", for shovel, the sapper's role is to shore up defensive trenches, build wells, telephone lines, and roadways, and provide other edifices and equipment as required by the army. It is hard work, and at Gallipoli the sapper is aided in his job by a team of sturdy mules, which carry material throughout the steep terrain. At times, the sappers build tunnels, or "saps" as they call them, right up to the enemy trenches, then it's a fun chase to undermine the enemy.

Philippe Barès, une lettre écrite dans un camp de prisonniers de guerre quelque part en Asie, mai 1915

Ma belle Marie-Hélène,

I don't know if you will ever receive this letter, or if I will live to hold you in my arms again. I write in part to absolve my guilt and in part as a gesture of defiance to gird me with hope. There has been little enough of that. Of my compatriots, the twenty-six men who put to sea under the command of Lieutenant commander Henri Fournier of the *Saphir*, I believe only a handful remain, although where they all are now, I cannot tell. My own survival, which I shall recount here, reads like a Jules Verne adventure, for the *Saphir* was scuttled by our own hands off the coast near Çanakkale, the citadel formerly known as Troy.

We were preparing to forge a path through the strait, as a needle leads a thread, so our allies might capture

Constantinople, but we had first to navigate the minefield laid in that channel by the Turks. Outside the boat, our crew members deflected two deadly explosives. Then something, to this day I don't know what, broke on the starboard side. The *Saphir* was taking on water. Whatever it was that came at us boomed and chortled as it invaded us. I quake still to think of its glee at discovering us.

Then the bilge pump failed. In that moment, I did not think I would live to see the end of the hour. But Fournier, blessed with a spine of steel, reminded us that we were not dead yet. While we tried frantically to mend the pump, the commander led us through enemy waters. For five long hours we limped along the seafloor. When he was sure we'd cleared the mines, Fournier cleared the ballast, but seawater rushed back into the bilge and we tilted. The pressure was too much. There were leaks everywhere.

The *Saphir* was sinking. The old girl moaned as if she knew it.

Worse, should the water reach the sub's batteries, we'd be overcome by poisonous gas. To save our lives, the lieutenant blew the security seals and dropped the anchors to catapult us to the surface.

Marie-Hélène, je te jure, nous sommes tombés de Charybde en Scylla.

No sooner had we breached the surface than we were ravaged by Ottoman guns from three Turkish gunboats. Fournier had saved us by sheer guts, and in different circumstances the *Saphir*—under his guidance—might have limped to safety, but we were flanked on both sides, and the gunboats were closing in. Of course, we could not have the Turks claim the *Saphir*. We had to scuttle her. We raced those gunboats to the deep water, where Fournier screamed at us to save ourselves.

I scrambled up the tower and onto the hull. Gods, but the water was blue.

When I leapt into the sea, I didn't expect to live. I recall the shock even now. The water was frigid. Gunfire blasted overhead.

We struck out for the shore, but François, my young friend, had never learned to swim. I tried to hold him, to drag him away from the foundering submarine, but his panic was like that of a feral cat. He scratched and clutched at me, even as I tried to save him. Pray for my soul, my love, but I kicked him forcefully in the chest, and swam away from him. He flailed a moment, then slipped quiet beneath the icy waves, his eyes accusing me even as the water claimed him. It's a sight that haunts me still. What could I do? We were a mile from land. I could not hope to save myself and save him, too. But perhaps François was the luckiest of us because he did not see what followed.

My gaolers come. I must hide this letter . . .

Cassius Smythe, journal entry, [illegible] *1915*

John, I met today with Chaplain Dennis McAdam of the army's chaplain department and had the esteemed privilege to spend some time in his company, observing him as he went about his daily chaplaincy work. It was not the Sabbath, but McAdam's first task of the day was to conduct a small service to mark the burial of a Private Flynn, just nineteen years old, who was killed in a recent *enfilade*, a lucky bullet piercing his neck. Only two of his comrades were in attendance, the same pair who had dug Flynn's grave, and the sole survivors of his unit not gravely wounded in the aforementioned fusillade.

The burial was a solemn affair, nevertheless I got a sense of the deceased man. Born and raised on the South Island settlement of Oamaru in New Zealand, it seems Flynn was liked by all those he encountered. He was a bit of a cheeky character, according to his friends, always quick with a joke and generous with his opinions. He was loyal and fair, with a strong streak of pragmatism, borne out in his stoicism when faced with his own mortality.

"Not to worry. It'll be all over soon," he'd choked out, even as the blood spurted from his neck in great gluts.

With no coffins to be had, the friends had sewn him into his greatcoat, his collar brought together at the edges in a zigzag. The lads thought Flynn was Presbyterian, but they couldn't be sure. McAdam assured them that it didn't matter. He said any man fallen in the service of his country would certainly be granted entry to heaven and his sins forgiven.

It was a short service. For all that McAdam had presided at the graveside of hundreds of men by now, the sentiment of his sermon was far from trite, and at one point I was moved to tears. When McAdam had concluded his eulogy, one of the lads recited a poem. After that they shook the chaplain's hand by turns, thanked me for bearing witness, then quickly set about filling the grave. A good thing too, as sniper fire had been zinging just beyond us throughout the sad proceedings. By the time McAdam and I moved on, after gingerly waiting out a respectful period, the pair were already heaping some larger stones over the grave.

"So many young men cut down before they've had a chance to live," I remarked. "Do you ever despair, McAdam? Even you must wonder at times if God has abandoned his disciples?"

McAdam grinned. "Not at all," he replied. "I think *God* is here and working harder than ever to protect the men." He nodded in the direction of an Indian soldier, who was urging a mule up a gnarly slope. "Every man's god is here. On both sides of the trenches."

It was a strange comment coming from a Christian chaplain, and I said as much.

"I wonder what the losses might be if God or Allah

were not here in such force," McAdam said by way of explanation.

I frowned. It was hard to imagine that the deaths to date had been curtailed in any way; the losses had been unfathomable, with men heaped hastily into mass graves sometimes without the benefit of even the few words that Flynn had just received.

"I have seen such acts of kindness and sacrifice that prove His presence to me," McAdam said.

I nodded. I, too, had heard many such accounts.

"And those gracious acts are not limited to our Allies. Our enemies have also shown compassion," McAdam said.

I looked up at that and my surprise must have shown on my face because McAdam went on, saying, "I wrote a letter home for a lad some days ago. He'd been discovered in a sap a day after the Turks had abandoned it; they'd dressed his wounds and given him water, without which he would certainly not have survived."

I thought on that while we shared a meal of biscuits and tea, after which I waited while McAdam stopped by the dressing tent to chat with the injured and to offer encouragement to a handful of exhausted stretcher bearers.

Later, we were proceeding up the hill towards Quinn's Post, dodging in and out of alleys and saps, when a man walking in front of us jolted then crumpled. Straight away, I threw myself against a wall, but McAdam, without thought for his own safety, went into action, running forward at a crouch and dragging the man into a nearby dugout. Sadly, the sniper had done his work and by the time I joined McAdam, there was nothing more to be done for the lad. The unlucky soldier's corpse was loaded onto a mule by a sapper and taken down to the lower slopes for burial.

McAdam poured water from his canister to wash the blood off his hands, and we continued on in silence, both somewhat rattled by the event.

After a spell, I said, "And if I were to turn my earlier question around? If you believe God is here and working hard to save the troops, do you also believe Satan is at work?"

He slowed at that and gave me a hard look, his grey eyes grave. "Yes," he murmured, and his eyes slid away to some unseen horizon. "Satan loves war. He is most certainly here, Mr Smythe, and whipping up disgruntled ghosts until they fairly froth for his cause."

"I believe you are a poet, sir."

The chaplain snorted. Leaning against the wall of the sap, he took out his daily quart of water again, this time taking a long drink. He offered the canister to me, but I shook my head, not wishing him to deprive him of his ration.

"Evil has ways of hiding, I think. Perhaps that is my own failing as I'm accustomed to look for God's hand in things, but it is also a chaplain's job to listen, so I know there are men here who are foundering under Satan's influence, men with black hearts, who take pleasure in cruelty, who show contempt for others' suffering."

It was the kind of answer one expects from a clergyman.

"Yes, callous men exist everywhere," I said, and, John, I could not help but think of the contempt my father showed me even as he showed me the door. We have not spoken since, and I suspect he has forbidden my mother and sister from contacting me. I believe he would welcome it if I were to die here.

I was brought back to the moment by a slap: McAdam squashing a fly on his neck, his hand coming away to reveal a streak of blood. "I believe other evils exist, too."

I looked up, my heart trembling at the turn in the conversation. "What evils, Chaplain?"

The chaplain sighed and wiped his palm on his trousers. "I don't know. I'm just a humble chaplain from Gisborne. I do not have the answers. But I am persuaded that this devastation cannot be solely the work of men, or even Satan. There is more at play."

Much later, when we parted company, the chaplain bade me seek out a Māori man by the name of Henare, based with the Wellingtons, who was purported to be something of a prophet.

"He may have the answers you seek," McAdam said.

Cassius Smythe, excerpt of an article in the Daily Star *characters of the campaign series, 1915*

THE ARMY CHAPLAIN
AT YOUR SERVICE

Army chaplains provide an essential service here at the Dardanelle Peninsula, where the spiritual welfare of the Empire's soldiers is paramount. It doesn't matter your preferred denomination, everyone is welcome to attend the Sunday service of army chaplain Dennis McAdam, held not in an elegant church erected for that purpose but in the open air with only an upturned biscuit tin as an altar. Attendance at the divine services is voluntary, given the many pressing tasks assigned a soldier, but those who attend appreciate the opportunity to maintain the spiritual learning begun at home, as well as the vital fellowship on offer, says McAdam, one of thirteen chaplains providing solace at Gaba Tepe. McAdam declares that he likes to keep the content of his sermons cheery. Outside of service times, the chaplain is kept busy providing succour to the injured, writing letters to families, and offering words of comfort to grieving comrades. Of course, there is the very sad task of presiding over burial services to our brave heroes fallen in the line of duty and called to their Eternal Home, a task which Chaplain McAdam says is "an honour".

Cassius Smythe, journal entry, June 1915

I sought out the Māori soldier, John Henare, as McAdam had suggested. He is a handsome fellow, dark as a Turk, and despite the outlandish content of our discussion, I liked him a lot, John, although I confess, I may have been influenced by his first name. I cannot quite explain it, but he conveyed a rare honesty as if he truly believed everything he said. I only wish I did not believe him.

"McAdam said you might come," Henare said, gesturing for me to take a seat on a crate. The cadence of his speech was broken and fragmented.

"The chaplain said you were something of a prophet," I said when I had settled.

The man shrugged. "We Māori call them *matakite*." He pronounced it mut-ah-key-tay. "People who can see the future and who speak to the gods." He thought for a moment then added, "Our Māori gods."

I nodded. "Can you tell if we will we prevail here?"

"We?"

"The Allies."

Like any soothsayer, his response was cryptic. "No one wins here, Mr Smythe."

"That's not what I mean—"

"Many will not leave this peninsula, including you and I. We will be devoured by *taniwha* sent by ancient gods." He had the strange habit of looking at the ground, as if he were reading the answers traced in the dirt.

I felt a spike of fear. "Taniwha? What is a taniwha?"

"They are serpent monsters. Demons that lurk in rivers and caves."

"And you think your New Zealand taniwha-demons exist here in the Dardanelles?"

"Not New Zealand taniwha. The monsters we face here are the demons of this place."

I confess that my head hurt; it was so much to take in. "How do you know all this?" I asked him.

He took a deep breath. "I know this will sound strange to you, but a morepork owl, a harbinger of death, spoke to my wairua-spirit before I left Aotearoa-New Zealand. It was December, when the *pōhutukawa* were flowering. The morepork said I would die in a place called Chunuk Bair."

Really? A little owl told him? It whispered in his ear?

John, I almost scoffed, but it was the man's religion

after all, so I was careful to keep my expression neutral. However, the fact that he mentioned Chunuk Bair, a hill here on the peninsula, was frightening. I decided it was most likely an error. He had mistaken the date. Even in England, there had been no talk of a land campaign in the Dardanelles before February. As for the hill of Chunuk Bair, which scarcely merited a dot on the map, Henare did not impress me as a liar, so I assumed he had likely heard of it since he arrived here.

"Tell me this, Mr Henare, if you knew you would die here, why would you come? You and your Māori compatriots had to make a petition to fight for the King. Why do that when you could stay safely at home?"

"It is a good question, Mr Smythe, and I have asked myself the same thing many times. In truth, I do not think a man can outrun his fate, and a warrior's death is an honourable one. As for my compatriots, I wish I could save them, but although we will lose many lives while trying to take this hill, the *mana* and prestige of the people of my country will be proven for all time."

"You're here for the honour?"

Henare chuckled. "Isn't everyone?"

"I don't know. Is there even such a thing in war?"

Henare studied the ground again. "Another good question, Mr Smythe."

The things I am learning, John . . .

Cassius Smythe, excerpt of an article in the Daily Star *characters of the campaign series, 1915*

BARBARIANS AT GALLIPOLI

The New Zealand Māori soldier is a sturdy fellow with a broad face and broader back. In ancient times, these men were formidable warriors, and now they are eager to serve, petitioning Major-General Sir Alexander Godley, commander of the New Zealand Expeditionary Force, for the right to fight for King and Empire. After some reflection, Godfrey took the natives' petition up the line to Prime Minister Massey who, faced with a keen need for troops, supported the establishment of a native contingent. It was a sound decision, as a more loyal soldier than the Māori one cannot find. Some at home in England may have witnessed their war dance, the haka, ahead of The Natives' rugby games against Britain. It is commonly agreed that it is a fearsome spectacle. The Turk is sure to run home in terror at the sight of it.

Philippe Barès, une lettre écrite dans un camp de prisonniers de guerre quelque part en Asie, peut-être juillet 1915

Cherie,

At last, I can resume this letter, which my captors must not find.

The Turks interrogated me again. I won't lie: their questions terrify me more than their cruel punishments. They do not ask about codes, or supply lines, or troop numbers as you might expect. Instead, they ask me about that day, about what I saw as I trod the cold waters of the Dardanelle Strait, after François was sucked into his watery grave.

I will tell you here what I will not tell them.

A sea monster claimed two dozen of my comrades. You will think me addled. Yes, I believe you will run your hand across my forehead and tell me to hush. You will coddle me with excuses, reminding me of the cold, of the enemies' shells striking the water all around us, our shock at losing the *Saphir*, or even my guilt over poor François, but I was not the only one to see it. Near on two dozen souls watched as the mist closed in around us, bizarre since just minutes before the day had been calm and the sky clear. We stopped swimming because we could no longer see the shore. We bobbed there inside the fog, a cluster of desperate men, frozen on the open sea.

Suddenly, the water stretched around us, swirling and eddying as if a whale were rising beneath us and was about to breach. Beside me, Patrice cried out, his voice full of terror. I could barely see the man for the shroud of fog, but guilt-stricken from the loss of François, I snatched at the air and caught him by the tunic, pulling him backwards and stroking hard with my other arm to get away, my legs burning despite the sea's glacial temperature.

All at once, a pocket of air cleared around us, as if we were suspended in the eye of a storm, and my feet found purchase. For a moment, I thought a miracle had happened and an island had chosen this moment to birth itself from the sea floor.

Instead, my blood clotted in my veins.

I was teetering not on a mountain summit but on the precipice of hell: the upper lip of a sightless sea creature. As I gazed down on its giant maw of taloned teeth, rows and rows of serrated daggers facing inwards, several of my wretched compatriots washed by me, carried in by the sea which cascaded over those deadly barbs in mesmerising ripples. I watched, paralysed, as my friends slithered down that gullet like raw oysters.

A tentacle, thick as a man's torso, brought me back to myself. It whistled by me, striking Patrice. I grasped for him a second time, but already he was falling, tumbling into that putrid hellhole. Desperate, he twisted as he slid, clasping at a curved tooth with both hands, the rasped edges slicing his palms and dousing his face with blood. It was a kindness that he did not see the monstrous tongue curl up from the depths to loose him like a piece of spinach from the tooth. The monster flicked him upwards, and he flailed in the air a moment, his face frozen in a rictus of terror, before the sinuous rope of mottled flesh curled tight around him, his insides oozing out over the coils. Patrice made no sound at all. Then its tongue snapped back, the creature dragging his remains into its sucking gullet.

I was not the sole witness to these events. There were others, evidenced by a moan, a curse, a mumbled prayer. I did not wait to count the survivors. I dived away with all my force. Not a second too soon. In that instant, the colossal maw closed and, at last, the monster breached. Marie-Hélène, it was gargantuan. As high as the *Tour Eiffel*.

I swam, flailed. When it crashed through the surface, I was pushed sideways on its wake, the spray blinding me. My eyes cleared to see the monster gobble up a comrade in a single gulp. I saw no one else. Was I the last? I girded my bowels, sure that my time was come, when one of the Turkish gunships appeared, grey upon grey, inside that brooding ring of fog. The Turks must have spied the monster's silhouette moving in the mists because there followed a hail of gunfire. The sightless creature turned its maw toward the sound.

The gunship couldn't turn. At least, not as quickly as that dreadful serpent.

I was grateful for the water in my ears which blocked out the worst of the men's screams. I did not linger to know the outcome. I could not see the shore, but I swam for the fog, hoping the obscurity might hide me. I swam like I had never swum before. I didn't look back.

Finally, I emerged from the fog and spied the cliffs. By now, I was exhausted. I kept you in my mind, *ma cherie*, as I made for the shore. So far away. I floundered for hours in that desolate strait, or at least it seemed that way. At times, I almost wished the monster would eat me, so acute was my distress. When my hands and feet were numb, and I feared I would perish from the cold, a Turkish boat appeared before me. *La France, mon pays,* please forgive me, but I lifted my hand and called for aid, and the Turks hauled my frozen body on board, their guns trained on me. I discovered three of my fellow crewmen huddled on the deck like living corpses, all trembling with cold and shock. The Turks fished up a further three before heading for shore. Lieutenant Commander Fournier was not among them.

So now you know how I am come to be still alive and mouldering in this stinking POW camp. Or perhaps I am dead, and this lonely stone cell is my personal purgatory for what I did to François, and for failing to save Patrice. Yet every other day the Turks haul me from my misery to question me about the events in the strait, so maybe I'm not so mad after all. I let them think I am, rolling my eyes and speaking in hushed tones of black fog and demons.

There is talk of an escape. A plan whispered through the walls by desperate men. I do not dare write it even here. If there is a way, I swear, I will make it back to you, *mon coeur*, to you and to France. I only hope I have not lost my mind.

Je suis toujours à toi,
Philippe.

———

Cassius Smythe, journal entry, June 1915

The days blur in a sleepless stink of heat, flies, wounds, dysentery, and interminable noise. I sincerely hope you are faring better where you are, John.

The stench, if not the flies, is much improved after the 24th May Armistice, which I assert was the most bizarre day of this campaign to date. The Turks called for a day of truce in order to clear the rotting bodies, several thousand from both sides, which littered the space between the trenches. From 7:30a.m. to 4:30p.m., nine glorious hours, the cove was quiet for the first time in many months. The respite from the noise was a blessed relief. Many of the troops took advantage of the ceasefire to enjoy a swim in the bay without risk from the snipers' persistent barrage. I was sorely tempted to join them, but the opportunity to report on such a historic event as the armistice, including seeing the trenches on the front line without risk of enemy fire, was too much for me and I ascended the hill with some of the other pressmen.

I have no words to capture the wretchedness of the scene between those limp white flags. It was unspeakable. Were it not my job to report the news, I would wish to expunge it from my memory.

In short, the dead lay where they fell, two and three and four deep in places, so you could not tread for fear of stepping on some poor sod. Their faces were disfigured, their bodies blistered and bloated. Some were so charred and blackened that their own mothers would not recognise them. Decaying limbs fell away from the bone like tender-cooked chicken. The smell was as thick as gravy. As were the flies. Many of the men could not bear it and ran from the field. Of those who stayed to complete the grim task, none were unaffected.

Nevertheless, the *détente* was cordial. Not a single shot was fired. Men from both armies mingled as if they were allies, offering cigarettes, food, sharing photos of wives and girlfriends, and other memorabilia of their respective homes.

John, I was able to speak first-hand with Jacko (a name affectionately afforded the Turkish soldier)—a rare opportunity. The man's actual name was Berat Aydem, and I later learned his first name translates as "the night of forgiveness" in Turkish. We spoke in French, or rather I did my best to communicate in my hesitant schoolboy pidgin. Berat, a linguistics professor before he volunteered, was rather more proficient, and where I did not know a word or phrase in French, he supplied an equivalent in German or, occasionally, in English, and by that manner we got by. For brevity, I record the essence of our conversation here, without those linguistic stumblings.

"That boy." He pointed to a corpse slumped over a scrubby bush of thyme.

"You knew him?"

Berat nodded. "A former student from some years ago. A very clever young man. He had a bright future before him."

It did not need to be said that the boy's future would now be nothing more than a shared grave on this desolate peninsula, and without even the dignity of a headstone.

"Did he have a family?" I asked.

The professor offered me a drink from a canister. "A mother and a father, surely," he replied when I had taken a gulp of water and handed the canister back. "As for whether he had children, I don't know. Not yet, I think."

We stepped aside to let two men pass, a stretcher slung between them loaded with decaying flesh. I covered my nose.

Berat waved his canister over the scene, like a priest offering benediction. "The loss of this one young man is bad enough, but a whole generation of scholars have been lost to this cursed paddock," he said. "Among those who survive, how many do you think will go back to their studies after this?"

"It is hard to calculate the losses in those terms," I agreed.

"The prophet urges men to seek out knowledge. To read and reflect. That is how we get closer to God." Berat took a breath. "This war . . ." He trailed off.

"I'm not sure God has a hand in anything that goes on today, Berat," I said softly. "Yours or mine."

Shaking his head, Berat glanced over to where the German commander Von Sanders was conversing with his Turkish officers, and lowering his voice, he said, "Allah forgive me, but certain officers are generous with their sacrifices of our Turkish sons."

I used the ruse of offering him a cigarette to turn my back to the officers. "At least he is on the field," I said. To my knowledge, Hamilton hadn't yet stepped foot on the peninsula. "It is harder to send men to their deaths when you must watch them do it."

Berat refused the cigarette. "Not so hard when those countrymen are not your own," he said bitterly. "Ten thousand Turkish sons shot dead. Wave after wave of them. Slain mercilessly. Ten thousand mothers will mourn."

My head whipped up at that. Ten thousand men, Berat had said. I scanned the field. We had buried hundreds, even thousands, but *ten thousand* on their side alone? There were not that many bodies.

No long after that, we shook hands and parted ways, Berat stooping to lift his former student and carry him to his final resting place. For myself, I had had enough of the waste, and I returned to my dugout near the beach. At the time, I put Berat's estimate down to exaggeration, but what reason would he have to lie to me? Later, when I thought on it, I wondered what had happened to those five thousand missing bodies. Had the scholar simply got the number wrong? Or had some other force claimed them?

I declare my imagination is running away from me, the effect of pungent gases and the excess of heat on that awful hillside most likely, although certain days it is not so hard to believe that higher forces underpin this dreadful campaign than the hubris and cruelty of men.

Cassius Smythe, journal entry, June 1915

Not wanting to let the story go, I went back to speak again with the sappers, Nichols, Tait, and Walters. I found them leaning against a bank of sandbags, smoking, their faces gleaming with sweat. I asked them about the reports of missing men.

Nichols guffawed. "Listen, Smythe, these hills here are riddled with tunnels." He pointed to my boots. "There's one right there where you're standing. We've built saps that pass under Jacko's trenches, sometimes less than five feet from where the enemy sleeps and eats. We only have to cough to bring the whole damned peninsula down on us. Add to that the shells and bombs exploding everywhere . . ."

Shifting uneasily from one hip to another, Tait spat a gob of phlegm on the dirt and took a long draw from his cigarette.

"God bless 'em, but the navy's aim is crude at best," Walters replied, lifting his chin towards the coast. "Of course we've bloody lost men, Smythe. It's a stupid question. We're working at speed and under fire. Tunnels collapse all the time . . ."

I shuddered at the thought of the poor souls buried alive in tunnel-graves they'd laboured to build. "And how many would you estimate you have lost?"

Rolling his eyes, Nichols puffed smoke. "Can't rightly say. Would you like us to dig them up and count them?"

"No, no of course not," I said hurriedly.

I headed back towards the beach.

When my back was turned, I heard one of them mutter, "Idiot," although I cannot say which.

Cassius Smythe, journal entry, July 1915

We are surely in Dante's Plain of Fire: blazing sand, constant fire, festering bites, and boiling streams of blood. . .

Cassius Smythe, journal entry, July 1915

John, one of the war correspondents, newly arrived in the Dardanelles, was recently at the Western Front. I have asked him about the state of things there, knowing that you are somewhere in the trenches. He is a reserved man with a softness to his voice that reminds me of our old house master, Houghton, although the reporter was of slender build, almost insubstantial. He put me in mind of the willows that we lay under that summer we picnicked next to the Avon. I suspect that ambiguity will serve him well if he intends on slipping in and out of the front lines. My heart swelled when he said he'd crossed paths with your regiment in France. He spoke of the valour and the loyalty of the 7th, both traits I associate with you, and I wondered then if perhaps if you'd seen him, or he saw you, and neither of you knew it. I take comfort in the possibility.

Cassius Smythe, journal entry, July 1915

There is a boy who wanders the beach here at Anzac Cove. Still in his teens, I'd wager. I was writing up some observations from an interview I'd taken with a stretcher bearer one morning, and I'd paused to watch while the boy gathered stones and lobbed them into a hole he had dug in the sand. The times his aim was true, and the stone landed in the hole, he burst into a fit of giggles. I'll admit, the first time I heard it, it lifted the hair on the back of my neck, although he is harmless enough, I think. I enquired about him of one of the men.

"Noah Walsh is his name," my informer said. "Great lad. Brave as hell, he was, but as yer can see he's mad as a hatter these days."

"Is he ill?"

The man rubbed at the bristles on his chin. "You could say that. Poor bugger. We had him lobbing bombs across No Man's Land into the Turk trenches, from the saps, or wherever the strip was narrow enough. You've got to have nerve to do that, and young Noah was bloody keen. He had a real knack for it, too. Got the distance right, and the timing, and, as you can see, he managed to keep his hands and fingers intact. He even jumped on a few that landed on our side and chucked 'em back. Damned effective, if you know what I mean?"

I nodded. By now, I knew that there were different types of bombs. Quite the industry, most of the bombs hurled at the enemy were made on the beach at Anzac Cove from spent cartridges and used jam tins. Of these, percussive bombs exploded on impact, whereas others operated on a time delay. The Germans (and Turks) favoured the latter variety.

"Did he take a hit to his head, then?" I asked.

The informer sniffed. "No, nothing like that. He got a bit trigger happy and started chucking bombs left, right, and centre. Mostly over the parapet. But there are limits, aren't there? The way he was going, there'd be none left if we got word of a big push. One of the officers put him right. Told him he had to stop. That's when he snapped. He took to throwing tins of bully beef over the top. You can't be throwing away food. After that, the officers ordered him off the front line."

I looked down the beach at the man, still lobbing stones in the hot sun. "He shouldn't be here."

"We all know that."

"Why doesn't someone do something about getting him sent home?"

The man spat on the ground. "Because there isn't a scratch on the lad. If the army sends him home, every man and his dog will be digging holes on the beach and lobbing stones into them, won't they?"

The sadness of Noah's plight tugged at my heart, so after the man left, I went down to the beach to chat with him. Staying well back behind the sniper line, I introduced myself and asked where he was from.

"Ireland."

"I hear it's pretty nice there," I said. I'd never been there myself, but almost anywhere was nicer than here.

Another stone landed in the hole, and, true to form, Noah let out a cackle.

"What are you up to there, Noah?"

He bent to pick up a stone and sidled over to me. "I'm bombing the bejeezus out of them, sir."

I assumed he meant the Turks, since my source had said that had been his job, but Noah put his hand to his mouth and leaned close. "The demons," he whispered conspiratorially. "They come in the smoke. They're after our souls, see? They want to suck us down the sinkhole straight into hell."

I shivered in spite of the heat. It was ridiculous. My imagination was so overblown with the testimonies of McAdam and Henare that I was giving credence to the words of a madman.

"It's a game, isn't it?" Noah went on, "to see which side will win. They can't even wait 'til we're dead, the sneaky bastards."

John, it was cruel to goad him, but the reporter in me couldn't let it go, much to my shame. "What can we do about it, Noah?" I asked.

The boy pushed away from me, smiling coyly. "Don't you worry, Mr Smythe. I'll get them." He opened his palm and showed the stone. "I've got this bomb, haven't I? I'm going to throw it in the pit and blow 'em to smithereens."

Cassius Smythe, journal entry, [illegible]

Here, in the following pages, is an account of my discussion with Nurse Mary MacLean, whom I met briefly on the *Maheno*, the New Zealand hospital ship, which was bearing some 400 wounded from Anzac Cove to the field hospital on the island of Lemnos, and whom I sought out again the following day on the pretext of an article about the dedicated work of the nursing divisions and the desperate need for medical supplies from allied governments. It was scarcely before six when she emerged for our interview. At that time, the first pink rays of the sun were peeking over the mountains, and already the night's cool was dissipating, although a grateful breeze flapped the nearby canvas tents. When we spoke, Nurse MacLean had not slept in many hours. Indeed, given her pallor and the tiredness evident around her eyes, I suspect she had not slept at all. Her apron, worn over her wool uniform, was spattered and stained. I carried her a cup of hot tea, which she accepted with gratitude.

"I cannot spare much time," she said, and her eyes strayed to the tents, from whence the moans of broken men calling pitifully for their mothers carried to us. "I am to begin my shift in a half-hour."

I nodded, and gestured to a spot further up the hill, away from the stench of putrefaction and antiseptic, and we took a seat on the ground overlooking the cove, where only the occasional shriek of some poor man pierced the morning quiet. In other times, the view would have been spectacular, had the ruts and scars caused by the movement of the troops and the general weary stain of the war not corrupted it. Nevertheless, a faint rose hue glinted on the water and, across the cove, the brown hills were serene in their slumber.

"Please inform your colleagues at the press that we need everything, Mr Smythe," Mary MacLean said by way of introduction. "Already, we are run out of the most rudimentary provisions. If we are to save these brave men, then we need bandages, antiseptic, blankets, soap. Fresh food. Even clean water is in short supply. How can we hope to nurse these poor men to vitality, how can we send them home to their families in any kind of health, when we are without the most basic of supplies?" Miss MacLean took a sip of the tea. She closed her eyes briefly, her eyelids fluttering, and I imagined her savouring its flavour, weak as it was.

I took the opportunity to study her. I guessed her to be in her late twenties. She wasn't handsome, but nor was she especially plain. Her face was round, and a pair of dimples suggested a ready smile, if there had been anything amusing to laugh about. I wondered what had prompted her to leave her home and come to war. A desire for independence? A thirst for adventure?

She opened her eyes and her face flushed. I pretended not to have witnessed her unguarded moment, choosing instead to scribble a note in my journal. "Blankets. Soap . . ." I murmured. The shortages were well known; water chief among them. I had sacrificed some of my own allocation for the mug of tea she held in her hand.

"How do you do it? Tell the things you know?" she asked.

I hadn't expected her to interrogate me. "I . . . I . . ." How could I confess to her that I do not tell the half of it? That even before the censor's pen, my words were twisted and truncated and full of omissions. It was as if every story I sent was stuck with a bayonet, drained until only a trickle of blood leaked, so the people at home, so England and her allies, could not suffer the truth of it.

Mary seemed not to notice my turmoil, or perhaps she was too consumed by her own. "I knew well enough what I was walking into," she said. "I knew that war was not all glory and medals. I was in Egypt before this, and that was bad enough. But the things I've seen here, Mr Smythe, they're almost too much to bear. Men so broken in body and mind that it might take the rest of their lives to repair—that is, if they repair at all. Those who survive arrive off the boats ravaged and rotting and crawling with maggots. I have seen men with their faces blown away, their limbs detached, and their innards belching. They come to us with their bodies slick with blood. Many of them will never walk again, will never see, will never father children. Many more have lost their minds from the horror."

She drank again, and I thought perhaps she was done, but she spoke again. "Do you know what galls me, Mr Smythe?"

"What is that, Miss MacLean? The futility? The waste?"

"Yes, those. But mostly, it is their unerring gratitude. I do nothing to merit it. Did you know the men refer to the nurses as angels from heaven?" She laughed softly, but her tone was bitter. "The men I minister to treat me as if I am their saviour, when all I can do to make them comfortable is dress their wounds, say a prayer, and move them on. The army crams those poor souls onto transports, one on top of the other, hoping they might survive, at least until they reach the next ill-equipped weigh-point on their journey home. Those are the lucky ones. The others, those hale enough to stand on two feet, we send back to the trenches for another round." She trailed off; her chin lifted to the mountains.

I brushed the grit off my page and lowered my voice. "I understand how you feel. All I do is report the news. At risk of my soul, I sometimes wonder if God has forsaken the men here."

"Or the gods," she replied. "We are not so far from Thessaly."

I cocked an eyebrow. Miss MacLean had a knowledge of the classics.

"You know, I once nursed a man who believed we are the playthings of the gods, that the divinities' desire for blood has nourished their pets and kept the underworld supplied with misplaced souls. He insisted it was the very reason our countries are converged on this hateful peninsula."

I lifted my head, drew in a breath of salty Aegean air, and waited.

Clasping her fingers around the empty mug, she clucked her tongue. "I've said too much."

"Not at all, Miss MacLean." I kept my gaze on the horizon, but my heart pummelled my ribs with machine-gun fire. "Stories are my passion as well as my trade. If you have the inclination, I would love to hear the tale."

"You'll think me fanciful as it is a tale to rival Mr Melville's."

I could not help but chuckle. "I'm a lover of Barrie's work myself. Besides," I said, and I waved my hand about me, "a little harmless fantasy is warranted given our circumstances, wouldn't you agree?"

She placed the mug on the dirt and crossed her legs. "His name was Foulard." She dropped her eyes. "Pierre was his first name. A Frenchman, he was one of my charges. I was the only one on the nursing staff with any French, and since few of the soldiers spoke to him, I sat at his bedside of an evening to take the edge off his loneliness. He'd fared better than some; he'd lost a foot and both his hands, not in the fighting, but because he'd spent too long battling the cold waters of the strait."

It was not so surprising. By now many ships and subs had been lost to the freezing waters, casualties of the enemy's torpedoes. More surprising was that the man had been plucked alive from the water.

"He told me that after his submarine sank, he swam a half-mile to shore, then made his way fifteen miles along the coast on ruined feet, travelling mainly at dawn and dusk, ducking inland only when absolutely necessary to avoid the enemy. When he slept, he did so upright, in crevices in the cliffs. He reached the mouth of the Dardanelle Strait two days later and took to the water again, allowing the current to carry him out to sea, where he was picked up by one of our transports."

"An elaborate fiction, surely."

"Perhaps. Any rescue is miraculous in these times. Although how he arrived at the field hospital is of no consequence; I had no reason to doubt the veracity of who he was. Not only did his uniform mark him as a member of the *marine nationale*, but he also wore the national identification wristband issued by the French navy, his name and the *Saphir* embossed on its face."

"His story would appear to be true, then."

"The rest is less readily verified: Pierre claimed to have seen a sea monster in the strait. He said the creature devoured an Ottoman gunship. It ate his compatriots, too."

"And you believed him?"

"I did, actually. I still do, in spite of my vocation for health science. Pierre declared he had seen the monster with his own eyes."

"You don't think his conjuring a monster was meant as a metaphor for the atrocity of war?" I thought of Henare, and of mad Noah on the beach.

"He said otherwise," Miss MacLean replied, "although he did not expect me to believe him, either."

"Hypothermia, perhaps. Or memories distorted by pain and loss. Given your account of his adventures, even you must admit it is a possibility."

"It's true that our memories are fickle, Mr Smythe. I'm contrary enough to hope that when I leave here, mine own will be distorted, the edges smoothed and softened so only moments like this one, of the two of us chatting on a dawn hillside in the Greek isles, might surface."

This time, it was I who flushed. Gallant, she flicked a fly off her skirts with her fingers to spare me embarrassment. "Nevertheless, I believed him. There was an honesty to his *récit*, a certain directness. You, as a of purveyor of language, will understand when I say that he did not once make use of the conditional or subjunctive tenses of his native language, and the intricacies of his tale, vivid and monstrous as they were, remained constant on retelling."

I stilled, feigning nonchalance, as I did not want to appear too eager. "What details in particular?" I said eventually.

"A serpentine monster, 100-feet long, with mouth-parts like a shark, its appearance preceded by a black mist."

My heart fluttered. "It *ate* the submarine?"

"No, not the submarine. Pierre said the *Saphir* was compromised, leaking on account of the mines. There was no way the sub would make it safely back, and they couldn't relinquish her to the enemy, so they had no choice but to scuttle her. No, it was a Turkish gunboat that succumbed to its coils. When the *Saphir* was forced to surface, Pierre said they were fired upon by *two* Turkish gunships, only the monster crushed one and consumed the escaping crew."

There followed some small talk about Melville's *Moby Dick*, and a discussion of the sad ratio of nurses to casualties, which I concede were as daunting as those faced on the slopes of Gallipoli. I promised to send a letter to my editor addressing her concerns.

At that point, Mary looked furtively around us. Apart from a handful of nurses scurrying between the tents below, there was no one near us, at least none yet awake. "Mr Smythe," she said softly. "Before you go, could I beg another favour of you?"

"Of course, Miss MacLean." I prayed she would not ask me to use my influence to locate some proof of life of a brother or lover doing his duty for the glory of the realm. She'd been so frank in her testimony, I could not countenance doing the same, being forced to reveal to her that her beloved was somewhere on the scrubby slopes of the peninsula drowned in his own blood, or swallowed by the mud into the very depths of hell.

Instead, Mary MacLean pulled a pair of scissors from the pocket of her apron and handed them to me. Then she slipped off her cotton nurse's veil and dropped it in her lap. Tangled brown tresses fell down her back. She gathered them in her hands. "If you would oblige me," she said. "It's the heat and the flies. The spurts of blood and vomit. With the lack of water even for drinking, I cannot hope to keep it clean. It simply isn't practical."

I got to my feet and, taking up the scissors, I bent over her, cutting off her hair so it was cropped close to her skull. It was close to 6:30a.m. when she replaced her veil and we parted ways, the strands of her brown hair lying on the dusty hillside.

I did not return to the island of Lemnos, and I did not see Miss MacLean again after that day.

The London Daily Times, *January 1915*

Lieutenant Henri Fournier, commander of French submarine the *Saphir*, failed in his attempt to repeat the heroic exploits of Britain's Lieutenant Commander Holbrook and his B11 submarine, who chased and destroyed Turkish battleship the *Messudieh* in the Dardanelle Strait as recently as December of last year. Fournier was able to successfully navigate the *Saphir* through various mine fields but for unknown reasons came aground near Çanakkale, where the sub was attacked by two Turkish gunships. Twenty-six members of the crew took to the sea, but the honourable skipper perished with the vessel. Survivors are believed to have been captured by the Turks.

Cassius Smythe, journal entry, August 1915

For two days I turned stretcher bearer, water carrier, letter writer while the dead rolled off the precipices after the assault of Chunuk Bair. There were so many grievously wounded that the stretcher bearers barely got halfway up the hill before they would have to carry someone back, most of whom died *en route* to the dressing stations. Hundreds are laid out on the beach waiting for transport, calling for water, for aid, for news of friends, for the release of death. Freezing or feverish, many have had their wishes granted and died where they lay. Many more, they tell me, gurgled and choked on the heights of Chunuk Bair.

The New Zealand machine gunners held the hill for three days. Reinforcements, sent to relieve the exhausted men, held high ground only another day before relinquishing it to the Turks.

I asked about John Henare and was told he is dead, cut down near the top, while fighting valiantly as he predicted. They say his body lies in a shallow trench somewhere, covered by the corpses of his compatriots.

Later, when I tried to catch an hour's sleep, I remembered our conversation.

"Many will not leave this peninsula, including you and I," Henare had said. "We will be devoured by *taniwha* sent by ancient gods."

The thought unnerved me, making me restless despite my exhaustion, so I got up and took myself back down to the beach to read to the injured men.

The assaults were over, but scores of wounded still waited to be evacuated, the shore strewn with rows upon rows of them, pushed as close to the cliff as possible to prevent the Turkish snipers hidden on the hillside from finishing them off.

A stretcher bearer by the name of Bertie Stratford, whom I'd helped to carry a man down the slopes two days before, sat on a crate outside a dressing station. He was re-padding his blistered palm with a grubby bandage. He glanced up at my approach.

"Come down for some quiet, eh, Smythe?"

It was laughable. There is not a scrap of quiet to be had in all of the peninsula. The ear-splitting boom of the cannons might have slowed since the assaults, the chatter of machine guns and the boom of rifle fire had scarce abated.

"Something like that," I said, lifting my book. "I couldn't sleep, so I thought I might read to some of the men."

"Good of you," Stratford said, tying the bandage off and getting to his feet. He scanned the sea of injured men. "There's plenty here who would welcome a kind word." Then he moved off to join his weary comrades, who were ferrying the wounded men onto the trawlers and barges for transfer to the hospital ships waiting offshore.

Using the light of a nearby lantern, I read to the men from Mr L. Frank Baum's *The Wonderful Wizard of Oz*, a fanciful tale not set in this world, and as far away from the trenches as could be. I began at Chapter 6, with the tale of the cowardly lion, and read for perhaps an hour, my voice a quiet constant among the gunfire, the shouts, and the crash of the surf.

By the time I closed the book, several of the men in my vicinity had quietened into sleep. As I walked among the rows, passing out cups of water from a barrel, I saw one poor man had died of his wounds. I nudged him to be sure, then I lifted his greatcoat gently over his head, a signal to the medics and stretcher bearers of his passing. Tomorrow, they would remove the dead man from the line and bury him here in a mass grave between the hills.

"Is Jacobs gone, sir?" The speaker had not the slightest trace of a beard. Another who'd lied about his age at the recruitment office.

I crouched alongside him and tucked the woollen blanket closer about his shoulders. "Yes. I'm afraid so. Did you know him . . .?" I waited for the boy to supply his name.

"Arty Gilbert," he rasped. "I knew Jacobs a bit. Since we got here. We'd become friends. I'm the reason he's dead. He saved my life up on the ridge."

"Then he's not only a friend, he's also a hero."

"Jacobs is . . . he *was* a farmer, from Matamata. Never been out of the Waikato before this. I guess he'll never get back there again, either." Gilbert choked back a sob.

"Where are you from then, Gilbert?"

"Auckland."

I smiled. "Looks like you'll be heading back there too, just as soon as the lads can get you loaded on a barge."

"I'm not so sure. I'm pretty beaten up."

"Ah. The medics will have you fixed up soon enough."

"If you say so, sir."

The poor fellow was talking himself into the grave. He needed a distraction. I sat down on the sand beside him and, putting aside my book, I pulled my journal from inside my tunic. Opened it to a fresh page and took out my pencil. "Would you like me to write a letter for you? A note to your mother perhaps, to tell her you're on the way?"

Though deathly pale, Gilbert seemed to brighten a bit. "You'd do that for me?"

"Of course."

His mother's name was Daphne. "I'm coming home, Mum," he said as I scribbled down the words. "What an adventure it's been."

He'd been up on the slopes near Chunuk Bair—although he couldn't tell me exactly where—his division pushing up in behind the first wave of Kiwis heading for the top of the ridge.

"The land up there is all steep gullies and cliffs. Miles and miles and miles of it. And yet, you could cover the flat land with a handkerchief. We travelled on our stomachs, like weevils, while Jacko's bullets whizzed all around us. Some of the boys copped it on the climb. We had no choice but to leave them where they lay, hoping we might come back for them later. From the embankment, the Turks fired on us, bombed us, hurled grenades. More than once our lads hurled their grenades back at them. It was a grand old time.

"Jacobs and I were among the lucky ones who made it to the assembly point at Rhododendron Spur, where we were meant to wait for reinforcements, only they didn't come. The terrain or the Turks got in the way. Who can tell? Well, orders are orders, so we pushed on anyway, trying to take the heights, and doing our best not to shoot one another. That's when Jacobs and I got separated from the Aucklanders, the earth shifting under us, stones flying. We tumbled down a narrow gully and were buried in the shale halfway down. We lay there a while, arm's length from one another, panting and desperate to catch our breath, and thirsty as all bejeezus, although we'd lost our water by that stage. A little rest out of sight of Jacko, we thought, before we hauled ourselves, and our gear, back up the hill."

A coughing fit took Gilbert then. I kept writing, catching up, while we waited out the spasm.

When he continued, his voice was raw. "So after a time we dug ourselves out and started the climb back to join the others, only it was like running up a sand dune, the ground hollowing out around our boots. We sank to our thighs, sliding further and further down the gully, until only a sliver of sky showed above us, the drifting smoke blocking out the light like a strange black mist. It was if the earth meant to swallow us. By then, we were both getting pretty twitchy, I can tell you."

"'We have to get out of here,' Jacobs hissed at me. 'What if Jacko takes a look down here? We're going to be holier than Christmas.'"

"But it wasn't Jacko who found us." Gilbert breathed deeply.

I waited, my pencil poised.

"A giant worm slid from a fissure below us. A great white beast, thick as a fencepost, that swirled and flashed about us. I know what you're thinking, Mister, that we'd hit our heads in the tumble, or the mustard gas had pickled us, or maybe I'd knocked myself out and dreamed it all.

"Then Jacobs screamed, 'Look out!' and I knew it was real because we couldn't both have the same dream, could we? And if I had any doubt, it was wiped away when that worm coiled itself around my chest and started to crush me. I thought I would die. I had not a spoonful of breath left in me. But Jacobs wasn't having it. He lifted his bayonet and plunged it into the worm, fair diving down onto it, like he was a fisherman with a harpoon. The worm released me and scarpered.

"I was still filling my lungs when Jacobs made it back up the slope to me. The ground on the other side of the fissure was firmer, and by using his spade as an anchor he'd managed to haul himself back up alongside me.

"'We've gotta get out of here, Arty,' he said.

"We didn't dawdle. Taking the trail Jacobs had discovered, our guns in one hand and our spades in the other, we climbed that slope like a pair of mountaineers. Soon enough bullets were zinging overhead. It was like coming home. We were almost there.

"But that worm had had a taste of me, hadn't he? I felt it rather than saw it, surging up from below us under the dirt. It struck my side. I felt like I'd been torpedoed. I was on fire. I twisted and bucked. I couldn't get it off me.

"Jacobs could have run. The edge of the canyon was just above us. Instead, he turned and shot off his rifle. Must have clipped it because the creature slithered away. Jacobs sent his grenade down into the hole after it, covered me while it exploded. Risky, since it could have taken us both back down that gully, and we both knew I didn't have it in me to do the climb again."

Exhausted, Gilbert could barely speak now. "Jacobs was a corker: he hauled me out of the gully, staunched the bleeding, and half-dragged half-carried me back to the nearest dressing station. I kept telling him he should leave me, but he wouldn't hear of it. We nearly made it too, but fifteen yards out a stray bullet hit him in the back. Stretcher bearers brought us down together."

I leaned closer. Dawn was not far off; the bursts of gunfire, nearby and in the distance, were becoming more frequent.

"And now he's dead. If I make it back, if I survive, I'm going to visit Jacob's parents on the farm in the Waikato. Tell them how he saved my life. I bloody hope the brass give him a medal . . ."

Light broke over the hills then, and I could see what the darkness had hidden. The blanket I'd tucked around Gilbert was soaked with large splotches of dark blood, one corner dripping onto the sand, where it seeped quietly away.

Suddenly, Gilbert reached out an arm and grabbed me by the wrist. "Mister. Please. I've changed my mind. Don't tell my mother that. Tell her anything but that. Tell her I died quick. That I was laughing with my mates —a silly joke—and I caught a bullet off the hills. Let her think they buried me under a tree, and the chaplain read a verse or two, while my friends stood all around me. Can you do that for me, Mister? Please?"

I nodded. "Daphne Gilbert, Auckland. I'll tell her exactly that, Arty," I said.

The boy's lids flickered in what might have been relief and he closed his eyes, clearly worn out from the effort of speaking.

I saw then that the stretcher bearer, Stratford, was

back, looking wearier than ever. Had he been toiling all night? He stepped alongside me and lifted Jacob's great-coat to check his pulse. Then, having assured himself the lad was dead, he signalled a porter over to help him separate the body from the casualties.

Keeping their heads low, the pair hoisted Jacobs between them. "We'll be back for that one, in a bit," Stratford told me, tilting his head towards Gilbert.

"Gilbert? No, he's not dead. I was just—" But Gilbert's head had lolled to the side, his eyes glazed, and I knew that I was wrong.

With Stratford gone, I lifted the blanket away from Gilbert's body to cover the boy's face, and that's when I saw his wounds. I almost vomited right there on the sand. Burned in lines across his chest and thighs were deep welts, the kind an octopus might leave when coiled around a prey. Worse, a massive chunk appeared to have been *bitten* from his torso, leaving his organs exposed.

The London Daily Times, *August 1915*

NEW ZEALANDERS STORM CHUNUK BAIR RIDGE

After three days of fierce fighting, on the 8th of August, soldiers of the New Zealand Infantry Brigade took Chunuk Bair at the summit of the Saru Bair ridge, a vital position for the march on Constantinople. Observers say General Hamilton is highly satisfied with the efforts of the colonials, with the Australian contingent also winning through to seize the Turkish trenches at Lone Pine. Heavy casualties are reported on both sides.

Cassius Smythe, excerpt of an article in the Daily Star *characters of the campaign series, 1915*

THE STRETCHER BEARER

The stretcher bearer is a level-headed fellow, and one of a team of four steadfast young men who carry those wounded soldiers unable to walk from battle to field dressing stations for treatment, or to the beaches for evacuation to hospitals elsewhere in the peninsula. Working twelve-hour shifts on the steep slopes here at Gallipoli, sometimes toiling in the dark. S BR David Tanner from Australia's 7th Battalion says it's a task that requires stamina, with a man's palms and knees suffering the worst for wear by the end of the shift. The role doesn't come without risk. Our Allied commanders like to keep the Turk on their toes with unexpected skirmishes and *enfilades*, and since occasional casualties are inevitable, a stretcher bearer must always be ready to jump into action, often coming under fire themselves. "I've had a few near misses, I can tell you," says Tanner, whose team claim they once climbed out of a trench and into No Man's Land to snatch a wounded soldier from under the noses of the enemy. It's all in a day's work for these chaps. Ask any soldier, and he will tell you there is none so brave as the stretcher bearer, and nothing more uplifting than to see

their white armbands displaying the red
cross come over the rise and to know
help is at hand.

Cassius Smythe, journal entry, September 1915

John, I am retired to Imbros for a week now, suffering
from an enteric illness which has ailed so many on the
peninsula. Please, do not worry for me. I was anxious for
a time, but a little good food and sleep has done the trick,
and already I am much improved.

While I was convalescing, I took Ashmead-Bartlett
aside to discuss my theory, joining him at his table in the
shade one afternoon while the rest of the press conclave
were occupied elsewhere. It was as good an opportunity
as any. Either he would believe me, or I could attribute
my comments to the whisperings of a fevered mind.

As it happens, A-B was keen for news from the front,
as his letter sent to Asquith by way of Murdoch was
confiscated by the military. That should have been the
end of it, but it seems young Murdoch penned his own
letter, and the news is all over London, and travelled as
far as campaign HQ. Needless to say, it has placed A-B
out of favour with General Hamilton, who has clipped
his wings, confining him to Imbros.

I told him of the chaplain's tale, of the *matakite's*

revelations and his predictions for Chunuk Bair, and of the Cetus-serpent seen by Harding and Johnson in the aftermath of the HMS *Triumph's* scuttling. Although I did not mention the deranged boy on the beach, Gilbert, the sappers, or even Nurse MacLean, it was a long tale, but A-B listened attentively. To my great astonishment, he did not appear overly surprised by it.

"I had an inkling, Smythe," he confided. "This is not my first war. And you'll recall I was on the HMS *Majestic* when it sank just two days after the *Triumph*."

I rolled my pencil between my fingers. It had been a dreadful period for the Empire, with three ships sunk in two weeks. Reports said Ashmead-Bartlett, expecting the ship would be shot at, had slept on the upper decks to ensure his timely escape. Fifty seamen, crew of the *Majestic*, had not been so lucky.

"Taken out by the same U-boat," the newsman replied. "You couldn't imagine a captain being that lucky, could you?"

"Did you see the monster?" I asked.

"Not with my own eyes, although I have heard the rumours."

My heart shrank a little. He did not believe me. "Rumours?"

A-B poured a glass of wine and set it before me. "You and I know otherwise, of course, but what is the world more likely to believe, Smythe? That warring gods have made us their playthings? That the campaign is nothing more than an elaborate game of chess, with the gods battling it out to see which of their monsters can claim the most pieces from the board?"

"Yes, that's exactly why I think we should—"

"Yes, we could do that, Smythe, and while it might be the truth, proving it would be a battle as hard won as Chunuk Bair." He got up then and stepped around me, stooping to speak into my ear. "Best that we reinforce the whispers already circulating, those instigated by Murdoch and Bean and myself, that General Hamilton is an incompetent buffoon whose poor decisions have led to the slaughter of the Empire's finest, and all the while his advisors were too lily-livered to confront him."

"But—" I started to rise from my chair.

Ashmead-Bartlett settled me back with a hand on each of my shoulders. "One enemy at a time, Smythe. One enemy at a time."

He left me sitting there under the trees. He was right, of course. The important thing was to follow the course most likely to stop the campaign, to do whatever was needed to get the men and the ships away from Dardanelle Peninsula and the evil forces controlling our fates.

Cassius Smythe, journal entry, September 1915

I do not sleep much these days, John. It isn't the crack of gunfire, which I am dulled to by now, and nor is it my health which, while not yet fully restored, is much improved. Mostly, my sleeplessness is out of anxiety for you, my dear friend, as I have not received a letter since January. I tell myself that you are fine, just too exhausted to write, and we both know there is precious little to say that will not get us into trouble with the censors and more. Still, some acknowledgement that you are alive would be a welcome salve. With the news reaching us of last month's Zeppelin raid on London, I worry too about my mother and sister at home in Bexley Heath, and even my father, who I have forgiven for his lack of compassion, though hell must freeze over before he will forgive me.

Harriet Margaret Smythe, an excerpt from her personal journal, October 1915

Cassius! I knew it! I knew you would not leave England and not send some word for your most beloved little sister. Months and months without the smallest shred of news. No letter or telegram—just your columns in the *Daily Star*, which are addressed to all and sundry. Whatever your quarrel with Father last Christmas, I could not imagine you would punish me so. I have been beside myself with angst.

Then last week, I was at my bedroom window and I

spied the postman stop to deliver a letter, but when I went downstairs and enquired as to its provenance, Mother denied it. Of course, I knew her assertion to be false, since I'd seen the postman deliver it with my own eyes. She twisted her wedding ring, her gaze sliding to where your photograph once stood on the sideboard, and I knew it could only have been a letter from you. I was determined to find it. Careful to avoid her notice, I searched Mother's writing desk, the kitchen cupboards, Father's study, I even checked between the pages of the book Mother had been reading. I was like Conan Doyle's detective Sherlock Holmes in my sleuthing. It took me a week, but eventually, I found your letters in a hatbox at the back of the closet in the guest room. Six of them, all written in your familiar spidery scrawl, made worse by the War Office's chicken scratchings. In that instant, I didn't know how to feel. All this time, you'd been writing to us and yet I'd had no knowledge of it. I was at once angry at the letters being withheld from me and full of joy for news of you. My excitement won out, and I carried the letters back to my bedroom, resolved not to budge until I had devoured every detail. I was doing just that—chuckling over your comment about army biscuits being harder than paving stones, and your stoic little poem about the donkey's carrying supplies up and down the slopes—when I heard Father's shout from downstairs. His bellowing was so loud, I swear it shook the windowpanes. Leaving the letters on my bed, I rushed downstairs. Given his distress, I imagined the German

Zeppelins passing overhead, even though it was only early afternoon. But the source of his anger was me. Cassius, I'm so sorry. Not wanting to draw attention to my discovery, I'd removed your letters from the hatbox and hurried to my room clutching them to my breast. My anticipation was such that I didn't notice one of them slip from the bundle and flutter through the staircase spindles to land on the hall rug downstairs.

That letter was now in Father's hand.

He flapped the missive accusingly at Mother, his face as purple as a crocus, as he screamed, "I thought I'd made it clear that Cassius is no longer welcome in this house, and that includes his stinking letters!"

I couldn't believe what I was hearing. Heretofore, I'd thought Father's resentment had festered because you *hadn't* written, because there'd been no chance for the two of you to reconcile before you parted to report on England's exploits in the Mediterranean, but to learn that he'd forbidden Mother and me from having any correspondence with you? My knees almost crumpled at the shock. Then my anger welled, because between the two of them, they'd been keeping you from me, and I'd had no say in the matter.

I pushed the drawing room door fully open, my hand clutching at the knob. "Why?" I demanded. "Why is Cassius forbidden from writing to me?"

The look on Father's face when he turned; Cassius, I thought he would implode.

"Leave now, Harriet!" he roared. "This doesn't

concern you. Go upstairs to your room." He pushed me bodily into the hall and closed the door in my face.

It didn't concern me? Of course it concerned me! I'm a member of the family, am I not? My skin bristled at being treated like an infant, and I refused to go upstairs like a good little girl. Instead, I hovered in the hall, my heart hammering as I eavesdropped.

"Arthur, please," I heard Mother say, her voice so faint I had to press my ear to the door. "What does it matter now?" she pleaded. "So Cassius sent a few letters. He hasn't heard from that friend of his all year. So many young men have died already in this dreadful war. Surely, you can't begrudge me news of our son."

Father grunted, and I caught the swift slap of paper on wood. "You may claim him if you choose, but he's no son of mine. I wash my hands of him. He's not even man enough to put on a uniform."

"You don't mean that. Cassius is risking his life to record the Allied efforts for the *Daily Star*. It's important work."

A snort. "I prefer *The London Times*."

"Arthur. Now, you're being contrary. Did you even read his letter? Cassius says that that the strangest things are—"

"No, I will not read it! For God's sake, Emma, it's unnatural."

Unnatural. It's become Father's favourite word of late. It's what he said when I asked to work on a nearby farm in support of the war effort. Mr Hennessey said he would be happy for my help now that so many of his farm hands have gone to war. Two of the local girls I know are already working there. You remember Susie Jefferies and Jennie MacDonald? I know you'll remember Jennie because she was sweet on you before you went up to the university. They say it's muddy work, and hard, digging up beets, but it can be fun too. At least they're doing their bit for England. Father won't hear of me working, of course. He says it's unnatural for women to wear trousers and pretend to be men. I know it's churlish to complain since there are souls aplenty whose plight is worse than mine, but you wouldn't believe how tired I am of sitting at home and knitting socks. Still, in just four months I'll be eighteen, and I'll do what I want. They're building a munitions filling factory in Abbey Wood, and I plan to go and work there and have my own money, and Father won't be able to do a thing about it. Even though, according to him, the war will likely be over before the factory is completed . . .

"What about Harriet?" Mother was saying on the other side of the door. "She misses her brother. You can't keep him from her forever."

"That's exactly what I intend. Can't you see I'm trying to protect her from this damnable godlessness? We cannot allow her to be corrupted, too."

There was the sound of paper tearing, and Mother gave a little squeal. "No. Arthur, please."

"I'm sorry. I've made my decision. There will be no further discussion."

The fire crackled, and I knew then that Father had burned the letter and I'd never know what you wrote. I didn't wait to hear any more. I ran upstairs to hide the others. I won't say where I put them, in case someone reads this journal, but Mother says I was right to hide them. She says she remembers every word, anyway.

Cassius Smythe, journal entry, October 1915

Hamilton has gone, to be replaced by Sir General Charles Monro. It seems we are not done here yet. The plague of flies has gone too, replaced by the cold.

I sleep barely at all now, tossing and turning for hours in my bed, pestered by Henare's predictions and wondering if I will meet the same fate as the New Zealander. I fret about the taniwha-monsters he mentioned, an uncanny match for the sea creature described by Harding and Johnson, and also Miss MacLean.

"One enemy at a time," Ashmead-Bartlett had said. He's long since gone, his office as a war correspondent revoked.

I sat up in my cot.

If ancient gods were duelling for the souls of the dead, which gods were they? Were the gods of the land making war with those of the sea? Henare had spoken of *land* taniwha that hunkered in caves and caverns. Was that what had killed Gilbert? Or was his story no more than the ramblings of a dying man? Perhaps, fatigued as I was in the days after Chunuk Bair, I'd been mistaken, and Gilbert's wounds were simply the result of spraying shrapnel and an overactive imagination?

My skin crawled with apprehension. I needed to know.

It was early, around three a.m., when I left my dugout and crossed the beach, carrying a dead digger's shovel. Overhead, gunfire rocked the cove, relentless as ever. I climbed the narrow paths, zig-zagging my way to the front lines. I had taken the path this far only twice before, and one of those times had been during the burial armistice. I hadn't realised that the journey would be worse at night, the dreaded whistle of the guns unnerving in the darkness. Sniper fire zinged around me. Once, I felt a bullet graze my coat, and another time the blade of the shovel clanged when it met with metal debris. I drew in my breath and climbed faster.

It did not help that it had rained recently, making the trail slippery, especially in the open. I sprinted from point to point, resting under cover where I could, squeezing close to the trench wall to make way for the stretcher bearers, who worked all hours carrying injured men to the dressing stations. Hard enough for me, near impossible to travel at speed when you must manoeuvre the treacherous byways burdened by a 200-pound weight and under constant gunfire.

"Where are you off to, Smythe?" asked a man who

had stopped for a smoke, his body curved to the wall to conceal the red glow of the cigarette. An Aussie accent. I didn't recognise him in the gloom. There was a spatter of fire, and something struck only inches from my scalp. "Keep your bloody head down, mate," the man said. "You'll get yourself pegged."

I nearly lost my nerve, but I kept on.

I don't know how long it took me to ascend to my destination. Possibly hours, as it was a mile or so above the beach and on treacherous terrain, achieved through ravines and across cliffs. At last, I wormed my way beyond the trenches, crawling past the firing line, into what had once been a deep trench before the May truce, but was now choked with the putrefying bodies of the dead. Thousands upon thousands of corpses, men who had lived and laughed only weeks before. British, German, Australian, Turk, all sharing this grubby bed, covered by only the barest smear of dirt.

I slowed, my courage failing. The stench of death was pitiable, but I had come this far and was determined to see it through. So, taking up the shovel, I steeled my guts and lay face-down at the edge of the pit, where I began the gruesome task of digging, quiet as could be so any nearby enemy sniper would not hear my scrabbling over the din of the guns. I did not have to dig far before my eyes pricked with the fumes of decaying flesh. I gagged and vomited. There was little enough in my stomach, but I could not help getting some on my tunic. It was of no matter, since my own ejecta could not be worse than the gases emanating from that ghastly pit.

After that, I resumed my task, eventually uncovering the first softening corpse. Although the skull had collapsed, the dead man cast a grisly eyeball over me. I dug some more, and the cadaver shied away from me, shrinking into the earth. I dug faster, chasing the dead man deeper into the pile. The corpse slipped away. I chased it until I was leaning into the chasm, my torso suspended over the crumbling edge. In that instant, a former colleague's newspaper report of a murderer who thwarted constables by burying a dog in the grave above his victims popped into my head. Was that what was happening here?

My throat constricted, and I stopped digging.

The pit was the entrance. It made sense. No one would dig up these men. No one but me. It was the perfect foil.

All at once, my skin rippled with gooseflesh. I peered into the gloom as a mesh of tiny white tendrils, like sickly vines, rose from the ground and coiled about the limbs of the corpse, pulling it down. I thought perhaps that I had dreamed it, it sank so slowly, but soon enough the dead man had disappeared, sunk beneath the earth, although the vivid stench of rot lingered.

I jerked up, heedless of the snipers. *What the hell?*

While I kneeled there, my chest heaving with terror, a tendril of white, thick as a man's arm, burst from the underworld and grasped me by the ankle. Seized by a sudden elan of fear, I cried out. Panicked, I bashed at the tentacle with the shovel, hard as I could, then kicked it away. By now, my heart was booming louder than the *Lizzie's* fifteen-inch naval gun. The awful tendril withdrew beneath the rubble.

What had the chaplain said? Evil forces. Disgruntled ghosts whipped until they frothed with dark cause . . .

My body trembled. I knew now that Henare had been right.

Alerted by my shout, a sniper fired at me. He couldn't see me in the darkness, yet he managed to kick up the dirt around my legs. He might be lucky yet. I didn't bother to crawl. Instead, I flung the shovel in the pit and ran upright, bullets screaming around me.

"What the hell are you doing over there? Get down!" someone shouted as I dove across the scrub into the safety of a trench. A rain of fire followed me in. I didn't care. In that moment, nothing could terrify me more than the horror of that pit. I didn't stop. I ran blindly through the trenches.

"You look like you seen a ghost, mate," the man with the cigarette said when I dashed past, my feet barely touching the ground. His laughter trailed after me.

Cassius Smythe, journal entry, November 1915

The press corps were not permitted access to General Charles Monro, those few of us who still remained in the Dardanelles. A wise decision, perhaps, given the trouble caused at home to General Hamilton. At least Monro deigned to step foot on the beachheads, arriving in the bay in late October *for a full six hours*, time enough to see for himself what has transpired here.

I saw my chance and waited by the latrines, since even a general must take a crap now and then. I lingered half a day lest I miss him, all the while fighting off the flies and the stench. I should have worn a gas mask, the fumes emanating from that pit were so vile. However, my patience was rewarded when Monro appeared. And since I had handed the man a clean stick on his way in, perhaps he felt beholden to speak a moment with me.

He exited, grumbling, "Never in my life . . ."

"Yes, sir," I replied. "I believe that pit was described in Dante's nine circles of Hell."

He chuckled grimly. We removed ourselves from the worst of the stench, and I poured a cup of water on the ground, so he might wash his hands in the stream.

"Cassius Smythe, General. From London's *Daily Star*."

"I'm afraid I don't have time for interviews, son." He flicked the water off his hands and batted away a cheeky fly which had landed on his nose.

"Not an interview, sir. Nothing for the papers. Just a word."

Monro squinted against the sun, then nodded. "All right. I'll afford you a moment."

"You need to stop this campaign, sir. Evacuate those still remaining and do not send any more. Dark forces are at work here. There is nothing to be gained."

The general turned slowly to face me. "Nothing to be gained, you say. How long have you been here, Smythe?"

"Since April, sir."

"But with the press corps."

"No, sir. Stationed here at Anzac Cove. Save for a fortnight when I was ill and was removed to Imbros."

He paused then and looked me over as if I were a curiosity. "So you do not believe we can win through?"

I shook my head sadly and repeated Henare's words. "No one wins here."

Monro clapped me on the shoulder. "Honest counsel from a newspaper man. Now that is refreshing. Thank you, Smythe. I will consider your advice." And with that, he strode away.

Cassius Smythe, journal entry, November 1915

The infernal gods have assailed us with a storm. What began with rain has turned to snow and sleet, and to

add to our misery a bitter northerly chills us to the bone
. . .

Cassius Smythe, journal entry, November 1915

The rain did not relent for several days, and a week on I swear I am still damp from it. The trenches flooded, causing landslides and washouts, and many men were drowned. I went to look for the sappers, Nichols, Tait, and Walters, and was told Walters had taken a chunk of shrapnel to his stomach during a fusillade a month before. Nichols had been seen of late, shoring up a sap, but not since the storm. Tait was about somewhere, though.

I found him sitting outside a dugout, his back to the wall and his boots slick with mud, and there was a far-away look in his eyes—a look I've become accustomed to in recent months. I hailed him and he jumped, startled, then his eyes focused and he relaxed.

"Oh it's you, Smythe." He lit a cigarette and sucked deeply.

"I thought I'd check on the welfare of some old friends. They told me the news about Walters. I'm sorry for your loss."

"Nichols is gone, too. Drowned." He got up as if to go, then abruptly sat down again.

There was nowhere dry, so I hunkered beside him. "I'm sorry," I said.

We sat in silence, him puffing on his cigarette.

"I shouldn't have called you an idiot," he said.

"Please. It's of no matter now." I patted his arm and felt him tense. I dropped my hand.

More silence.

After a while, he said, "You were right about the tunnels."

What could I say? That I wasn't surprised? I picked the mud off my tunic and waited for him to go on. Minutes passed.

At last, he said, "When the storm came, Nichols and I were rushed in to shore up a tunnel that looked set to give way. Well, you know what it was like: we were up to our waists in water and frozen to the core, and half the time we were working blind, since the lanterns kept going out. It was a losing battle from the outset. The tunnel we were in, the timbers were creaking something terrible and the water was roaring. I was sure it was about to come down around our ears. There were just the two of us left, and I told him to come away, but Nichols was as stubborn as sheep dung, wasn't he? A deluge came through, a veritable wall of water and mud, and we were swept up in the freezing torrent.

"I was helpless. Like a leaf, the current carried me along. I was turned around and bashed against the walls. It was all I could do to suck in gulps from the pockets of air near the ceiling. Yet all the time, I was aware of

Nichols, fighting for breath alongside me. We both knew those tunnels better than we know our own mothers, so while we still breathed there was a chance, you know?" He trailed off. Took a deep drag on his cigarette. A curl of grey smoke slipped between his lips.

"Something took him. Something uncanny. I saw it snake across the ceiling. The wave had sent me tumbling, so I'd come up facing backwards with Nichols behind me facing forward. A pulsing white arm slithered down from the ceiling and curled about his neck. Tightened. Nichols' eyes bulged, and his hands went to his throat. I'll never forget the look he gave me. The arm or the tentacle or whatever it was jerked backwards, pulling him away from me, back into the tunnel against the current."

"I never saw him again. The tunnel has drained since. No one's found his body."

I didn't insult him with platitudes. I didn't move either, although by now my knees were aching.

"People get carried *with* the current, not against it."

I nodded.

"Smythe," he said, turning towards me. "If Monro insists we push on, how am I going to go back down there?"

Cassius Smythe, journal entry, November 1915

Two mail boats sank this past week, one leaving the peninsula, and another coming in. My letter to you is drifting at the bottom of the sea, John. Perhaps yours to me is there as well.

Cassius Smythe, journal entry, December 1915

General Monro has convinced Kitchener to quit the Dardanelles, and this is in spite of Admiral Churchill's grizzling. I felt a prick of pride when I learned the news, thinking that perhaps I had played a small part in securing that result. Now, every day, our Allied troops are shipped off this sorry coast by the score, even as the gunners keep up their shelling, a deceit to convince Jacko we are still in the game.

By rights I should be happy, and yet my heart is sore. The tide may be turning, but it is not fast enough. Men are disappearing from the cove, and not all of them on the evacuation boats. I am convinced the monsters suck them from their dugouts and drag them from the trenches under our very noses. It is more than I can bear.

I could leave now, of course; the *Daily Star* recalled me months ago, but there are too few journalists left on the peninsula for me to abandon my work. We in the press have a moral responsibility to tell the truth to the end, have we not? But what truth? I'll admit I am afraid, my beloved John, Henare's words haunting me yet. If only I were certain that you were dead, his prediction should not vex me.

Hope, I fear, is the cruellest thing.

Excerpt from a transcript of the editorial meeting between Daily Star *publisher Mr Alfred George Gardiner and his chief editor, Mr Alexander Jones, December 1915. The dictation taken by Mr Gardiner's secretary, Mr Geoffrey Smith*

Mr Gardiner: So, we have the report of the German cruiser sunk in the Baltic Sea; and, on the Western Front, Haig has replaced John French as commander of the British Expeditionary Force. What news from the Allied campaign in the Dardanelles? Do we have anything from Smythe?

Mr Jones: Yes, sir. After issues with the mail delivery last month—it seems numerous mail ships were lost—this month we've received two columns from Smythe. You won't believe it, but one of them contains not a single redaction by the War Office.

Mr Gardiner: That hardly seems possible. Did it miss the censors?

Mr Jones: No, sir. The censor's stamp is on the bottom right of the page, so it seems they have sighted it.

Mr Gardiner: Well, is it any good?

Mr Jones: It's more of the same, sir. Ghostly sightings and fanciful tales about demons and monsters. The War Office must have discounted it as a fiction, or perhaps a fairy tale of the kind Mr Lewis Carroll would write. *[Mr Jones handed Mr Gardiner Smythe's report. There's a pause while Mr Gardiner reads it.]*

Mr Gardiner: We need to get that lad back home, Jones. He's been too long out there baking under the Turkish sun. The man has clearly lost his reason.

· · ·

Mr Jones: I agree, sir. It's a damned shame. Let's hope he sees sense this time. We sent word two months ago that Smythe was to retire to England on the next available ship, that he has acquitted himself with honour where the paper is concerned.

Mr Gardiner: Indeed.

Mr Jones: Smythe rejected our request. He refuses to come home, sir. He claims he's collecting testimonies for a book which he hopes to publish after the war, true accounts from the people who know what is really happening on the peninsula. Even suggested the *Daily Star* might serialise it.

Mr Gardiner: Well, if he refuses to return, let's hope he sends us something we can publish, and not another character of the campaign, so help me God. But that still leaves us without a column for tomorrow's edition. We need to print something!

Mr Jones: Smythe did send a rather fine little poem, sir. A love sonnet. *[There is another pause as Mr Jones hands over a second sheet of paper for Mr Gardiner to consider.]*

. . .

Mr Gardiner: [reads] My heart . . . Did you know he had a sweetheart?

Mr Jones: No, sir. None of us here in the office had the slightest *soupçon*. Smythe always was a bit of a dark horse. He rarely joined us for drinks of an evening.

Mr Gardiner: And now we know why. You'd think he'd be keen to get home to her, wouldn't you?

Mr Jones: Perhaps the lass got tired of waiting and married another, sir.

Mr Gardiner: She wouldn't be the first.

Mr Jones: The war was supposed to be over by May . . .

Mr Gardiner: I like the poem.

Mr Jones: It is rather clever, a pressman's perspective, and it mentions the *Star*. I note *The London Times* gained a wonderful reception to Laurence Binyon's little poem last year.

Mr Gardiner: They did, didn't they? Let's run the poem, then.

Mr Jones: Of course, sir.

Mr Gardiner: Do we have the shipping logs for page 7...?

Poem by Cassius Smythe, journalist for the Daily Star, *published December 1915*

To the Aegean, guided by a *Star*
 In service of my king or feckless gods
 A conduit of hope sent from afar
 My great coat made of lies, I join the squads

And subsist in squalor on these arid hills
 Where mortal flesh makes war with flies and fear
 Empire, Ottoman, gluts of blood are spilled
 War's promised glory losing its veneer

· · ·

And though a pressman's meant to tell it true
    Lines are crossed, my words are contradiction
    The truth? With no one here to tell it to
    Men die and gods laugh with malediction

The truth then, is for each man to decide
    My heart, I'm truest when you're by my side

Cassius Smythe, journal entry, January 1915

John, soon my turn will come to leave this wretched place, although I have still so much to do. My pencil is kept busy, recording testimonies, seeking out those who know the terrible truth. No doubt the men think I am as mad as poor Noah Walsh, lobbing his stones on the beach. Perhaps they humour me out of kindness.

Yet, as the days pass, the Māori's forecast bothers me less. More and more, I suspect he was speaking in metaphor. After all, not a one will return home from this place the same man as he left. Perhaps that was what Henare meant when he said I might die here.

I wish I could be sure.

George Peter Edmunds, excerpt from a letter sent to his brother Frank Joseph Edmunds, February 1916

. . . it was a strange thing, those last days of the Gallipoli campaign. While we hated the place, none of us wanted to be away. There was a niggling reluctance to depart, despite the ongoing evacuation. I reckon it a cause of the dissatisfaction of not having won through after all we'd suffered here. They say some 100,000 are dead on this lonely peninsula. To think, I had never seen a dead body afore leaving home. Now I've seen more than I care to. So many lost, and what have we gained?

Apart from the gunners, who bravely watched Jacko while we boarded the barges, our company was among the last to leave Gaba Tepe. Our party included a journalist by the name of Smythe, who had gotten himself attached to us somehow. The men liked him well enough, probably because the man was free with his cigarettes. A civilian, he might have bugged out early with the other pressmen, yet Smythe remained behind. From what I could tell, he spent the last days of the evacuation in a dogged frenzy, going from man to man, seeking out our testimonies, and scribbling them down in his journal like some macabre speaker for the dead. When we asked him why, he said he wanted to bear witness to what had truly happened here. Who really knows what the truth is,

Frank? Still, I suppose one day people might want to read about what went on. It would take a gifted writer to conjure this hell. Those who fought here would prefer to forget it—if that is even possible. For myself, I am haunted by nightmares of friends riddled with bullet holes, now eaten by worms; that is, those lucky enough to rest in graves. Rest: now there is a fine thing. It is a relief to get some proper sleep before we are away to [redacted] for the next battle on behalf of King and country.

I'm getting ahead of myself. I was going to tell you about Smythe. It was because of the pressman's own determination to record the troops' stories for posterity that I recount this event from our last moments on the Turkish coast.

Throughout, we were trying to keep the evacuation from the Turks, getting the guns and stores away, and burying or burning any item of use we couldn't take with us. The evacuation took place over several weeks, and the night we pulled out, a fire burned on the beach, and the wind was blowing such that black smoke billowed at our backs and the surf rose up to meet us.

I was already on the boat when Smythe tossed his typewriter over the side, preparing to leap in after it. I stowed the machine, then turned to help him in as he was up to his thighs in the foam. All at once our Turkish hosts sent us a farewell salute, and shrapnel exploded above our heads. I ducked into my collar and saw Smythe stagger. I reckon he was hit, although I didn't see where exactly he'd copped it. He was standing yet, and weaving for the boat like a drunkard, but for a period he disappeared from view, obscured by a waft of smoke so dense I couldn't see my hand in front of my face.

Through the smoke, however, I heard him yell, "The black mist!"

I shouted at him to follow my voice, to get in the damned boat, for God's sake. Blow me down if the idiot didn't chuckle. Then the smoke cleared a bit, and I caught sight of him teetering in the water. He was pointing at something in the shallows.

"A dark shadow in the water, Edmunds. Do you see that? The monsters are not done with us yet."

By this time, the boat was pulling away from the surf, the lads keen to get us out of range of the snipers' gunfire. The journalist was in danger of being left behind.

"Smythe," I called. "Give me your hand, man!"

A white tentacle snaked out from under the boat. It darted towards Smythe and yanked his feet from under him. He cried out.

He was a yard beyond my reach, still I thrust out my hand. "Smythe!" I called.

If he heard me over the din of the surf, I don't know. The sinuous tentacle whipped back and twisted around his torso. His eyes widened.

Only then did he reach for me. "Edmunds," he choked.

The tentacle gripped him tightly, and he was pulled

under. I watched the ripples shoot away, dragging him under the boat. I ran the length of the craft, shoving men out of the way, calling for someone to grab a rope, but when I reached the bow, he was already too far away to save. Some kraken of the sea had claimed him. You'll think me addled in the head, and that may be true, since none of us who escaped that beach did not bear some demon or other, but I know this: he could not have swum under the boat that fast, not against the surf.

In the distance, Smythe raised his hand; I glimpsed it through the fog. Then he slipped beneath the surface and was gone.

The cheer didn't go up until we were into the open sea and out of reach of the Turk. We were free of the cove, at last. I never saw Smythe again. With the smoke and the spray, no one else had seen him fall. When I told my friend Arthur that Smythe had stumbled in the waves, he clapped me on the back, assuring me that he'd likely be picked up by one of the other boats, but we both knew there was little chance of that. Smythe is just another poor sod lost to this sorry war, and his death isn't even the weirdest I'd seen in these past months.

When we got to [redacted], I opened the beaten typewriter bag. Inside, I found his journal. A photo labelled John / Summer 1913 was tucked inside the front cover. A brother, or perhaps a friend. I've handed it all to the authorities to pass on to his employer.

Now we are awaiting transport to [redacted] from whence we will depart for [redacted]. It's as Father always says: no rest for the wicked. At home, the farm will be coming into the end of summer and the trees will be fruiting. I wish I could be home to see it. I will stop there and get this letter in the post. Please give my love to Wendy.

Your brother, George.

Alfred George Gardiner, letter to Mr and Mrs Arthur James Smythe of Bexley Heath, Kent, March 1916

Dear Mr and Mrs Arthur Smythe,

It is with my sincerest condolences that I return this typewriter, the possession of your most beloved son, Cassius Elgin Smythe. A dedicated employee, a fine young man, and an ardent patriot of the Dominion, Cassius was taken from us in a cruel parting blow imparted by the Ottoman Empire as the troops departed the Dardanelles. I am assured by a witness that it was a quick death, cleanly done, and that your son felt no pain.

That your son's body sleeps in foreign waters "beyond England's foam"[2] is a source of profound regret for all of us at the newspaper, who remember Cassius with affection and respect. However, please take solace in the knowledge that his was not a life wasted: Cassius's words are immortalised in his vivid and insightful descriptions of the characters of the campaign. Indeed, his writings, some of which have been published latterly in the *Daily Star*, have contributed greatly to the morale of our soldiers and their families.

I regret, however, that no other belongings can be returned to you at this time. Due to classified information contained therein, Cassius's journal, which I understand includes his observations and some draft writings, has been retained by the War Office until the conflict is resolved, which must surely be soon.

On behalf of your son's colleagues at the *Daily Star*, please accept our deepest condolences for his sacrifice, made in service of King George V and to the Empire.

Yours faithfully,

Alfred George Gardiner, Publisher

Laurence Binyon, excerpt from "For the Fallen", a poem published in The London Times, *September 1914*

"They went with songs to the battle, they were young,

    Straight of limb, true of eye, steady and aglow.

    They were staunch to the end against odds uncounted;

    They fell with their faces to the foe."[2*]

---

* 2. Laurence Binyon, "For the Fallen", *The London Times*, 21 September 1914, p9. https://www.poetryfoundation.org/poems/57322/for-the-fallen

Edward's Journal

I accept the package with trembling hands. Wrapped in brown paper and secured with string, my name is written in black letters on the front, the Y in Hennessey smudged at the top. I don't open it immediately, laying it on the sideboard while I go about my chores. Only when they're completed do I gather up the package and take it into the garden to open, away from the busy eyes of my sisters.

I sit on the bench seat facing the lane, where the scent of honeysuckle permeates the air, and prise open the knot to fold back the brown paper. My breath catches. There on my lap is Edward's journal, its brown leather cover stained, and its pages warped and dog-eared. A dull ache settles between my shoulder blades.

It's been thirteen years since I last saw it, the day he departed with the 57th regiment...

"Every man should have an adventure," Edward had told me, his grey eyes twinkling with merriment as he lifted me off my feet and hugged me goodbye. It hadn't been proper – I'd been barely fourteen – but being my father's favourite has its benefits, my father indulging us by looking away.

A swallow flits by, venturing out from its nest beneath the soffit. I watch it go, not ready to open the journal yet. Instead, I pull the crumpled letter from the pocket of my skirt, smoothing the paper out, and reading every word, although by now I know them better than my heart.

January 1861

Margaret, we are arrived this morning in New Zealand and await aboard for our orders. I admit to feeling no remorse at the prospect of leaving the Castilian *as I am no sailor. I do not know any among us who appreciated the incessant sway of the hull, the accursed creaking that robbed us of our rest, and the resolve of the cook to bore us senseless with the blandness of his fare. From where I write here on the deck, the port looks like any you would see in England, fertile and full of promise, although they say the terrain is deadly, and the natives, even our allies, are tricky devils. I do not say this to alarm you, darling Margaret, only to assure you that after our experiences in India, we of the 57th regiment are prepared for any challenge. If the Government wish us to enforce the peaceful* *settlement of these shores for God-fearing citizens, then we shall certainly oblige them. I shall not complain about the weather, though, which, while warm, is pleasantly cooler than Bombay...*

I smile again, remembering how Edward had never liked the heat...

Margaret, we were marched from the creaking timbers of the Castilian *to a place called Onehunga, which the locals pronounce Own-nay-hunger. A risible name, and a risible tale, since not hours after we arrived there, we were made to board another ship, the warship* HMS Cordelia, *from whence I am writing, in spite of the swell of the ocean beneath me. As I pen this, we approach Waitara near New Plymouth, and the start of our next colonial adventure. I am invigorated by the prospect. Already, I can see the mountain that towers over this region, a perfect cone arising from the peninsula; this glorious edifice is surely a beacon to the gods. If there is time, I shall put this letter with the Quartermaster to despatch on his return to Auckland. I send all my best wishes to you, cousin, and to my uncle, your father.*

Ever yours, Eddie.

· · ·

I hold the letter to my face and inhale deeply, hoping for a hint of him, or perchance a vestige of the ocean. Any such trace is long gone and instead I breathe in the lilac I use to scent my own clothes. This letter: the last to reach me, written on pages torn from his journal. For six years, I've waited in vain for another. Since then, there's been nothing but rumour, each one grinding away at my resolve, stripping me of hope. Had he been separated from his regiment? Could he be lost in that alien forest, turning in circles, unable to find his way? Perhaps he'd died in battle and lay buried under the mud somewhere, his bones slowly rotting while strange plants sprung forth to conceal his resting place. Certain mean-spirited souls whispered behind my back that Edward had been a coward who ran from a fight and was now too ashamed to return. They said he'd forsaken me, choosing instead to take a native to wife and live with her like a savage in the bush. Ignoring the eyes that slid away from mine, I paid no heed to the ugly gossip that drifted in my wake and, after a while, with no news to confirm or deny their validity, the rumours stopped.

A year later, Arthur Bearnsley had come courting. A decent gentle man with a good position, Arthur had been patient with me, but Edward was always in my thoughts. I kept him waiting too long for my answer and, in the end, pressured by his mother, he wed another.

No fretting over shed milk, Margaret.

I allow myself the luxury of a sigh, then, wiping my eyes with the corner of my apron, I tuck the letter back in my pocket. What would his journal reveal? I run my palms over the warm leather, dallying. It's strange: all these years I've longed for news of Edward, but now that I have his testimony in my hands, I'm afraid to open it. I do it quickly, selecting an entry at random...

4 April 1864

Margaret, I regret the poverty of my hand today, so childish I can scarce read my own words. In truth, I am trembling like a child. There are nine of us, separated from the first grenadiers. We are hidden in the bush after witnessing the very worst of humanity. I fear sharing this account with you, dear cousin, but we have always been frank, and if the words are too gruesome when I have completed the tale, as they surely must be, then I shall rip the pages from my journal and bury them in the scrub, for we cannot risk a fire...

We left early this morn from the redoubt at Kaitake. Taking the South Road, we were so buoyed with confidence and bravado, it is hard to fathom our departure was but hours ago. We were led by a man named Captain Thomas Lloyd, our mission the same as it has been for some time now, to burn or confiscate any crops and foodstuffs which might sustain the Māori. We were to badger the natives into moving off the land and going elsewhere, wherever that may be. The day was nothing unusual: fresh and misty with a tang to the air. Lloyd split the party in two near Te Ahuhu. I remained with the captain's party. I was pleased to do it. A tallish fellow still with a good head of hair and fashionable sideburns that conflated his beard, the captain impressed me as a decent sort, solid and fair, and perhaps not as impetuous as some others of his age...

Margaret, I am stricken: Lloyd was cut down in his prime. It was only by Providence that I was not with him, as I had needed a moment of privacy.

Those cunning Hau Hau, the so-called Christian Māori, had built a trench system, cutting their saps deep into the bank, invisible to Captain Lloyd and his party ascending the slope. The rebels leapt from the trenches, ambushing our front guard. One of their warriors, a fearsome man with scars across his chest, lifted his club and, with a single slice of that deadly blade, the captain's head was severed from his shoulders. Lloyd's white breeches did nothing to diminish the sight of his lifeblood pumping from that gruesome stump. There was so much blood. A river of treachery. Yet even in death, our noble Captain Lloyd fought on, his body twitching long moments on the ground.

In that instant, I avow, I did not go to my commander's aid. I was paralysed with fear. What advantage would there be in my dying too? So I stayed out of sight and bit my hand to prevent myself from crying out. It was well I did. Seven soldiers were killed. Decapitated. Dooley lost a leg, cleaved off with one of those flattened greenstone blades. That isn't the worst of it. Like vampires, the Māori warriors drank the blood of our comrades. I watched while Eastman, Dooley and Poole were exsanguinated, their blood drenching the warrior's bodies. It drooled from the side of the warriors' mouths and spilled over their chests.

Not an Enfield was fired. No word was spoken. When the Hau Hau departed, carrying the heads of our countrymen, the nine of us fled, bashing our way through the forest and into the hills.

My heart pounds, my chest tight with fear. Does he still live? I flick forward several pages, not to read them but to reassure myself that Edward had not perished that very night, perhaps overcome by the same Māori savages who had butchered his captain. To my relief, there are several more entries, somewhat rushed, but all written in Edward's familiar hand. Quieted, I return to the previous entry and, turning the page, continue my reading.

12 April 1864

Margaret, since Lloyd's demise, we remain hidden in the foothills, isolated from our compatriots, awaiting reinforcements, which must surely come soon. We are only seven now, two of our number killed when we attempted to return to the redoubt the day after Lloyd's death. Setting out before dawn, we travelled single file through the grey bush, silent but for the thud of our boots on the mud, and the brush of ferns on our shoulders.

Not one saw who attacked us, or even the hour they attacked, but when we stopped to rest, Jones and Giraldy were missing. We retraced our steps, anticipating a mishap. It was a strong probability: the terrain is treacherous here, dense and dripping, and full of unseen perils. A mile behind us, we found their boot marks, deep gouges scraped in the mud, and moss sloughed off fallen branches where they had been dragged through the undergrowth.

By now, Baxter had worked himself into a lather. His eyes wild, he said the men were lost, carried off by the murderous Hau Hau.

"That fool, Grey, expects us to treat the Māori as our brothers," he railed. "These thick-lipped people, who carve their bodies with chisels and knives, and adorn themselves with crude ungodly patterns. How can we trust savages such as these?"

McKenzie had scowled at that. It is widely known he is a sympathiser. The man keeps a native 'wife', even speaks the language. Under the circumstances, it was well he did not voice his viewpoint, because Baxter was not alone in his belief that the Hau Hau had returned to slaughter us while we were weakened in both spirit and numbers. Uneasy, the men murmured and shifted their feet.

"Does no one else smell a rat?" Baxter warned us. He said we should go back. "This piteous trail will only expose us to the same fate as our compatriots," he insisted. "We should make for the redoubt."

He turned to go, but Finnigan and Ilot wouldn't have it.

"They don't call us the Die Hards because we turn our back on our own," Finnigan said, his finger raised like my

old governor. Burly and thickset, Finnigan stands as high as a stallion with the muscles to match. It takes a brave man to stand up to Finnigan.

Baxter persisted. "We ran when they killed Lloyd," he said.

"That was different," said Finnigan.

Since Finnigan saved my life in India, what choice did I have but to agree? We set off, following the trail of desperate scuffs, Baxter reluctantly falling in behind us. Finnigan took the lead, cutting a trail through the trees as those calamitous tracks took us deeper and deeper into the forest. At times, the foliage was so dense and the mist so thick we could barely see in front of our faces; still, we pushed on. Then, without precedent, the scuffs stopped. Finnigan had us search the area for the men. With the dusk descending upon us, we checked every embankment, lifted every fern. Margaret, we scoured every inch, we found not a trace of them.

"The Hau Hau have them," Donaldson asserted.

We others could offer no more plausible explanation. Giraldy and Jones were lost. Even Finnigan was forced to admit it. Worse, in searching for the missing men, we'd lost our way, like Grimms' tale of Hänsel und Grethel. Ilot disagreed, assuring us that all was well, that if we kept our current course we would meet the trail again, that we might yet encounter the garrison search party sent to fetch us back. His confidence was met with uneasy glances. Still, what other course was open to us? So we trusted to God, and to Ilot, and trudged on, each keeping an apprehensive eye fixed on the bush. My skin prickled, the hairs on the back of my neck lifting. Shivering, I imagined watchful eyes observing us from behind every twisted tree.

I'm determined now that it was nothing, just my predilection for fanciful thoughts.

Take, for example, this occurrence during my voyage on the Castilian. It was the strangest event and yet, at the time, I was convinced of its veracity. We'd been at sea for several days and, feeling feverish, I ventured onto the deck in search of fresh air, and perhaps in the hope of seeing land on the horizon. No one accompanied me; the squalls on deck were brisk and bracing, and lashing rain made the deck treacherous. You mustn't scold me, Margaret. I was not at risk, taking care to hook my arm about a stay to secure me to the ship, for the seas were vigorous. The sails flapped and the Castilian groaned, the vessel cresting a swell the size of a small mountain. On the descent of that formidable wave, through the swirling winds, I bore witness to a monster of the sea. I blinked, knowing I was mistaken, that it was a drifting log, or perhaps the mast of some unfortunate wreck, and yet the image persisted, as clear as a daguerreotype. The monster, for I can call it nothing else, was a serpentine beast of 200 feet. Dark-skinned and spotted, its head was the size of a barrel and bore a strange wrinkled crest on its forehead. Translucent, the monster rippled beneath the swell, a noiseless Stygian creature beside the Castilian. I had never been more pleased to stand on the solid timbers of the ship. My heart thundered like hoofbeats and my knees shook. I was bewitched, unable to look away despite my desire. Instead, I squinted against the rain to study it. For a harrowing moment, it too considered me, the malevolence in its yellowed eye forcing the breath from my lungs, but then the Castilian *shuddered and rose again, and the creature disappeared into the inky depths.*

For days afterwards, nothing had been truer: I was persuaded I had witnessed a monster of the sea, such is the extent of my imagination. Every time my thoughts strayed there, the monster became larger, clearer, more omnipresent, my fertile mind ever aggrandising it in the manner of a hapless fisherman describing his elusive catch. Of course, there was nothing there. The beast was conjured from my mind. The storm was the cause, or else the apparition was a manifestation of my high fever. And the same must have been true as we, the survivors of the 57th, marched onwards, because when we set up our camp near a small crick in the darkness several hours later, we numbered seven, sound and whole.

"Margaret!" my sister Evie calls from the back porch. "Mother says you're to come in for supper." While I've been reading, the afternoon sun has seeped away above the hills. I will have to continue my lecture later. I tuck my letter in the journal to mark the page, wrap the book loosely in its original brown paper skin and hurry inside.

It's much later, in my room, candlelight flickering

against the walls, that I am able to return to Edward's missive.

Margaret, we awoke to a strange ululating. I jumped to my feet, my musket at the ready, and peered into the trees, but could see no one. Tense moments passed. The threat, had there been one, was gone. All around me, angry gazes were directed at Ilot, our sentry for the small hours. Ilot only shrugged. A little way off, Finnigan gave a shout.

"Giraldy iss back," he said.

We jumped rotting logs, trampled low bushes, in our haste to reach them. It was Giraldy, but he was barely recognisable: supine on the muddy ground, he was tinged blue and enveloped from head to toe in thick gelatinous slime. Opaque and criss-crossed with white filaments, the glutinous cocoon put me in mind of a frog's spawn with its gelatinous covering, or perhaps a spider's prey, wrapped for consumption at the creature's leisure. Inside his filmy wrapping, Giraldy jerked. My skin crawled.

"He's still alive! Help him!" Finnigan urged.

Shaking his head, McKenzie handed me his blade. I dropped to my knee and, grasping at the mouldering jelly, sliced away the mucous obstructing Giraldy's mouth, praying that the man might suck in a breath and be revived. Sadly, his chest did not rise. He did not jerk again.

"Here, let me," Finnigan said, pushing me aside and taking up the blade. The pair had been friends, neighbours since their youth, so his grief was palpable.

Scraping away the remaining mucous, Finnigan uncovered Giraldy's face. I staggered backwards, repulsed.

Gibbous eyes stared out at us. Globes of terror, in a visage that was burned away, the raw tissue pink and oozing. A glob of slime slithered down his cheek.

Margaret, I shall report the words that passed between us, but you must forgive their coarseness, for our distress was extreme.

His fist clenched, Big Finnigan shook with fury. "Bloody brutes," he whispered.

Baxter sneered. "Those fucking Hau Hau!"

But McKenzie shook his head again. "This isn't the work of the Māori," he said.

"What do you know?" Baxter interjected. "You think fornicating with one grants you admission to a native's mind? Ha! You flatter yourself if you think your member reaches that far. It's of no matter, their women cannot be trusted any more than the men. Sly creatures with the devil's mark on their chins, they're little more than beasts!" His face was pale, and beneath his arms his tunic was stained with sweat. His chest heaved as if he had just run to the docks and back.

"But where is Jones?" Donaldson asked.

At that, Creighton turned and vomited in the bushes, although what he had to purge, I cannot imagine, there had been little enough time for eating since Lloyd's death. Creighton's reaction brought me back to myself. My hands were burning where I had grasped the slime. I rushed for the crick and plunged them in the water, only emerging when I had rinsed away the gelatinous ooze and the smears of Giraldy's blood.

. . .

13 April 1864

After burying Giraldy's corpse, we marched less than two miles before stopping to rest, our nerves frayed and our spirits weaker than a tumbler of McClintock's ale. The ululation came again, unholy high-pitched notes that chilled us to the bone. Baxter said it was the bloody Hau Hau, trying to steal us of our courage. McKenzie said it was a bird, a piriwharauroa. A laughing cuckoo.

Baxter had scoffed at that. In truth, I don't know what to believe, except when we clambered to our feet to press on, Donaldson had disappeared. We searched the site and found the drag marks, slithering off into the bush.

Finnigan hitched his musket over his shoulder. "We should follow them," he said.

"It's too late," Baxter countered.

Finnigan's jaw rippled. "He might still be alive. You saw what happened to Giraldy. If it were you, would you wish us to abandon you?"

It was a mistake to mention Giraldy. The man's fate was too fresh, the image of that glutinous coffin too gruesome, and the men all found something of interest on the ground.

"For Christ's sake!" Finnigan cursed.

"We can't keep doing this," Ilot whined.

"What do you propose?" Finnigan demanded.

"Make camp, set sentries, and wait for the garrison to find us."

"Ilot's right," Baxter said. "While we're on the move, we're vulnerable."

"What if the garrison isn't looking for us?" Finnigan asked, his voice soft for a big man. "What if they already reckon us dead?"

No one answered him, and the eerie ululation commenced again.

20 April 1864

I am ashamed to say that this morning one of our number left us, Margaret, taking his own life. Perhaps Donaldson is responsible, his body turning up at the edge of the camp yesterday, wrapped in its corrosive slime cocoon. Finnigan postulated that the shock of our compatriot's discovery overwhelmed him, although what other outcome did he expect once we spied the poor man's boot marks in the mud? I do not want to imagine what passed through Donaldson's mind as he was dragged from us through the undergrowth. What must it be like to be drowned in mucous?

"Why didn't he scream?" Ilot asked.

It is a question we have all been asking.

He had been gone six days, so Finnigan and I buried him yesterday without preamble. I concede the task was herculean. More than once I had to put up my trowel. These days, I am a new-born foal, my arms have gotten so spindly. Even standing is an effort: my legs wobble like an infant's. We are starving. Knowing something of the

Māori ways, McKenzie has foraged the nearby forest, but the sodden roots and berries he's found could scarce sustain a rabbit, let alone a group of famished men. I ate the fat white caterpillar he offered me, greasy saliva welling in my mouth as I swallowed. It was putrid.

Ah, Margaret, what I would not give for one of your scones now. My mouth waters at the thought.

It took the five of us the better part of today to bury the man who took his own life. I do not write his name here out of respect for what we of the 57th regiment have been through together; nevertheless, it is hard not to think of him as the lowest of men. Your father would surely deem him a miserable sinner.

Although, I hope Grey and his soldiers find us soon, because each night, when darkness falls with its shifting mist, and the unspeakable ululation begins again in earnest, I rather envy the sinner his slumber.

There is no need for alarm, dearest Margaret. I do not mean to kill myself. I only wish I could be gone from here, transported in an instant, back to England and to you, for New Zealand is the wildest, most desolate of places.

Do you recall my first impressions as I sat on the deck of the Cordelia *and admired the perfect cone of the mountain at New Plymouth? I felt certain the peak was intended as a beacon to the gods. You will forgive me if I laugh aloud, for I fear only Lucifer took up the call. We are surely in hell. For days we have been assaulted by a relentless, unpitying deluge. It is as if the mountain has captured the clouds, holding them against its flanks with the express purpose of torturing us. The forest that surrounds us is thick and dense, and water drips everywhere. Sometimes I wonder, was I ever dry? Then, there are the swarms of vicious black flies that consume the miserable flesh that remains to us. When the flies have supped their fill, fat welts rise at the site. We scratch at the bites with our fingernails, desperate to purge the murderous itching. It is enough to drive a man insane. Of all of us, McKenzie suffers the least, rubbing the leaves of a plant he calls ngāio on his skin. He claims it is an old wives' tale; a Māori remedy against the flies.*

The rest of us prefer to endure.

I look up. Dark shadows hover in the corners of my room. The house is quiet, the household long since gone to their beds. With bleary eyes and shaking hands, I turn the pages. Only a handful of entries remain. Dare I read on? No, I should wait until the morn, where the golden sunlight and smell of baking bread will dampen my fears.

Sliding the journal onto my nightstand, I pull my nightdress over my head and slip beneath my covers, reassuring myself that all will be well. Why else would I have received the journal? Edward will have sent it ahead to prepare me. Surely, he is safe in the garrison, yet weakened still from his ordeal. I must not fret because as soon as he is sufficiently recovered, Governor Grey will transport him back to England, *back to me...*

Morning is too far away. My candle is good for

another hour, so I lift the journal onto my knees and read on.

28 April 1864.

Ilot has gone and more drag marks have appeared only yards from where I slept. And always that damnable ululating. Incessant. On and on. Driving us to distraction. Finnigan and McKenzie are urging us to leave. Baxter refuses. We are too weak to withstand an assault, anyway.

Baxter said if the Hau Hau were to bring Ilot back on the morn, he might be tempted to eat him. A poor joke, but still we laughed.

"It isn't the Hau Hau," McKenzie insisted.

We shook our heads. What does he know?

Last night, when I slept, I dreamed of home, of the lane where I plucked a honeysuckle flower from the hedgerow and tucked it in your hair. Do you think of me still, Margaret? Will anyone read these words? Is it cowardly of me to admit I am too tired and too heartsick to hope?

30 April 1864

Somehow McKenzie's Māori woman has found us. She came creeping into the camp at twilight. Finnigan, jumpy as all hell, almost blew her head off with his musket. It was lucky he didn't because, wondrous of wondrous events, she brought with her a basket of sweet potatoes. I bit right into one, the rough purple skin included, eating the hard flesh as if it were an apple. My stomach has shrunk so much, I could only eat one, but I swear I had never eaten anything so delicious.

"Ask her when Grey's men will get here," Baxter demanded, his mouth full of the tuber.

McKenzie spoke to her in the skipping sing-song tones of her native language. The woman shook her head and pulled on McKenzie's arm, urging him to come away.

"She says we have to leave," McKenzie said. "We need to go now, tonight. She says unspeakable things dwell here. Evil kehua-spirits."

Baxter's eyes narrowed in suspicion. "Why is she here, then? Are the Hau Hau so impatient to wrap us in their slime-filled cocoons that they've sent her to lure us to our deaths?"

"No," McKenzie said. "She says the Hau Hau went east to the coast, taking the head of our chief with them. She says Governor Grey took the soldiers from the garrison and followed them."

Baxter cackled. "For someone not aligned with the Hau Hau, she knows a lot," he said.

The ululating started up, strident and melancholy. The woman's eyes grew wide. She tugged at McKenzie's hand, speaking quickly in his ear.

"Bad omen. I'm going with her," McKenzie said abruptly. "You can stay if you want."

"I'll come," said Finnigan. He grasped at a tree trunk, using it to support his weight as he clambered to his feet.

"She's with those butchers, I'm telling you," Baxter hissed. "She'll get you both killed."

Finnigan and McKenzie looked at me. "Chatfield?"

I wanted to go with them, but without Baxter? We were the 57th. Eleven years we'd been together, from Inkerman and Sevastapol to Malta and India, and finally across the world to New Zealand. Die Hards, they called us. Someone had to stay with him. Since Finnigan and McKenzie had declared they would go, there was no one else.

Finnigan saw me hesitate. "I'll send a party back for you both, he said. I'll do it the moment we arrive at the garrison. You have my word."

They departed before I had wished them Godspeed, the three of them turning and slipping into the bracken. All that remained of them were three small potatoes.

"Fools. The Hau Hau will have them. They'll be dead before daybreak," Baxter said.

I could only shrug. The odds were unfavourable, whatever the course.

In the morning, it was Baxter who was gone, the skids of his boots trailing off into the bush.

My candle flickers. Tears stream down my face.

Please, no.

.   .   .

I put the journal aside and wrap my arms around my body, determined not to read another word. But in the end, I do, if only to accompany him in spirit, because I cannot bear to think of Edward all alone.

May 1864

It has been four days, or is it five, since Finnigan and McKenzie left for the garrison. I have counted the hours, trying to determine when they might arrive. How long would it take them to find their way back? Three days? Four? How long to send a search party? Should I expect them soon? Baxter has been back since yesterday, wrapped in his glutinous casing. I can see his eyes bulging through the slime as he lies beside me. Sometimes, I see them follow me. I'd bury him, but I can barely stand. He's a quiet companion with his mouth full of mucous.

One moment, I fear no one will come for me, and then, in the next, I fear they will.

I'm afraid to fall asleep.

Well, I cannot complain for the lack of adventure. How many men can claim to have seen a sea monster? Although, if I had wanted rain, I might have stopped at home.

Speak to me of home, Margaret. I would hear about your day. Is the honeysuckle still in flower? What of your father? How was his sermon last Sunday? Did anyone snore? Of course, I am teasing. I'm sure it was very fine. I'm so very sorry I missed it. Perhaps I will be home for

Christmas. That is a blessed thought. But the light will be gone soon, so I will stop my writing now.

My fingers quake and I turn the page. Edward's last entry. The words leap from the paper, and I gasp, clapping my hands to my mouth. The journal clatters to the floor. It doesn't matter that I cannot see his hand, because I cannot unsee the words.

Margaret, the ululation. They're coming.

Afterword

Despatches began as an epistolary cosmic horror tale set against the backdrop of war, with the 1915 Allied campaign at Gallipoli providing the perfect arena for a plot involving Lovecraftian-type monsters and unfathomable horror. However, as is often the case with writing, the novella turned into something else—a kind of re-envisioning of the Cassandra myth, with my protagonist, pressman Cassius Smythe, gifted with a terrible knowledge but unable to tell it, since no one will believe him, or if they do, they must deny it. For me, the story became a study of truth, those versions we wish to reveal and those we feel we must hide, and it reminded me of a conversation I had with my mother once about whether or not we should use the "good" china. The old school of thought was that our best tableware should be reserved for honoured guests, while the cheaper everyday service would suffice for family and friends because the people who love us do so in spite of our flaws. But while writing the story, I realised that, in reality, we often hide our authentic selves from those we love the most, and not always in our own interests, but to spare them hurt. And I learned that an unacknowledged truth can be a heavy burden indeed.

For those readers who may be less familiar with Great War history, many of the events in the story actually happened, including: the 25th April landing day massacre; the Navy censorship of true accounts in favour of letters and articles purporting glory and success; the gruesome 24th May burial armistice; the heroic and deadly capture of Chunuk Bair by the New Zealand Infantry Contingent; and strong criticism of the military leadership of General Hamilton by the press which, when leaked, led to his replacement by General Monro and the eventual evacuation of the region. The Māori contingent did indeed petition Sir Alexander Godfrey for the right to join their compatriots in battle, later distinguishing themselves in the fighting, including at Chunuk Bair. The main Māori contingent, however, did not arrive on the Peninsula until July. The heat, flies, illness, and the November storm which appear in *Despatches* are also well documented in accounts. Also noted in the story are some of the ships and submarines lost throughout 1914-1916 on the Dardanelle Peninsula. Vessels mentioned in this story are: the Q44 submarine, the *Saphir*, which sunk in January 1915 in the Dardanelle Strait, and the HMS *Triumph* and the HMS

Majestic, warships which provided bombardment cover to the troops fighting on the coast and which were scuttled within two days of one another in May 1915 (Journalist Ashmead-Bartlett was among those rescued). Incoming and outgoing mail trawlers sank in November to the bitter disappointment of the troops and their families. However, while real events and some well-known historic figures appear in *Despatches*, unless specified, conversations reported in the story are entirely fictitious. Any factual errors in the text are mine alone.

Central to my research for this work was Glynn Harper's compelling book *Letters from Gallipoli: New Zealand Soldiers Write Home*. These candid letters, told in New Zealanders' own words, reveal their experiences at Gallipoli. The authors' accounts are highly moving. Sometimes, what is unsaid is even more revelatory. I highly recommend the text for first-hand accounts of the hardships suffered, and also the moments of courage and integrity. Ashmead-Bartlett's book *Expedition to the Dardanelles*, written after the fact, since his notes were lost in the wreck of the HMS *Majestic*, is also excellent reading.

Finally, observant readers may have noted the dedication for *Despatches* is to Leonard Machin Nicklin (Service # WWI 2/767), my adopted grandfather. Len was an old-school type, a gentle practical man, who walked four miles a day, always wore suspenders, a grey felt hat, and called my mother Mrs Thomas. A big part of my early years, he filled my brother and me with a love of books and history, even as he filled us up on home-baked madeira cake from a battered biscuit tin. He lived alone into his nineties, keeping a vegetable garden the size of a tennis court from which he fed half the neighbourhood. But long before I knew him and loved him as a grandpa, he was a driver in the New Zealand Expeditionary Forces, and stationed at Gallipoli, where he took care of the donkeys. I can still recall seeing his Gallipoli Medal which he kept in a special box. I remember his comments, both sad and bitter, about sniper fire on the beach at Anzac Cove, and his overwhelming gratitude for the nurses who cared for him later when he served at the Somme, France, where he lost one side of his face in a shell explosion, an event which ultimately resulted in his evacuation. His tales of the Great War, but more especially the quiet gaps in his tales, those long moments when he would trail off, his grey eyes filling with tears, have coloured this story. Len Nicklin is buried in Putāruru, New Zealand.

About the Author

Lee Murray is a multi-award-winning author-editor, essayist, poet, and screenwriter from Aotearoa-New Zealand, and New Zealand's Prime Minister's Award winner for Literary Achievement in Fiction. A *USA Today* Bestselling author, Shirley Jackson- and five-time Bram Stoker Awards® winner, she is an NZSA Honorary Literary Fellow, a Grimshaw Sargeson Fellow, and winner of the NZSA Laura Solomon Cuba Press Prize. Read more at www.leemurray.info

Also by Lee Murray

Taine McKenna Adventures

Into the Mist

Into the Sounds

Into the Ashes

Path of Ra series (with Dan Rabarts)

Hounds of the Underworld

Teeth of the Wolf

Blood of the Sun

Collections

Grotesque: Monster Stories

Penny Divers and Other Stories

Poetry

Fox Spirit on a Distant Cloud

www.ingramcontent.com/pod-product-compliance
Lightning Source LLC
Chambersburg PA
CBHW031307120726
47906CB00003B/929